FRANKIE

FRANKIE

J. Sydney Jones

LODESTAR BOOKS
Dutton   New York

to the sibs: Gwenyth, Creddwynn, and Lowell

Copyright © 1997 by J. Sydney Jones

Library of Congress Cataloging-in-Publication Data

Jones, J. Sydney.
    Frankie / J. Sydney Jones.—1st ed.
    p. cm.
    Summary: During the unrest created by the coal strike in Colorado in 1913–1914, Luke faces questions about this local happening while also dealing with his feelings toward a mysterious runaway.
    ISBN 0-525-67574-4 (alk. paper)
    1. Coal Strike, Colo., 1913–1914—Juvenile fiction. [1. Coal Strike, Colo., 1913–1914—Fiction. 2. Strikes and lockouts—Fiction. 3. Runaways—Fiction. 4. Interpersonal relations—Fiction.] I. Title.
PZ7.J72015Fr   1997
[Fic]—dc21
                                97-10197   CIP   AC

Published in the United States by Lodestar Books,
an affiliate of Dutton Children's Books,
a member of Penguin Putnam Inc.,
375 Hudson Street, New York, New York 10014

Published simultaneously in Canada
by McClelland & Stewart, Toronto.

Editor: Virginia Buckley   Designer: Dick Granald

Printed in the U.S.A.
First Edition
2   4   6   8   10   9   7   5   3   1

Acknowledgments

My name is on the cover, but many people helped carry the load. Howard Zinn inspired this book with his retelling of the Ludlow Massacre in *A People's History of the United States*. Dick Jackson gave generously of his editorial talents in early stages of the writing to give focus to the story. Tess Jones and Cheryl Gomez read initial drafts, refueling my enthusiasm with their own. And finally, my editor at Lodestar, Virginia Buckley, turned a manuscript into a novel. Her savvy suggestions made me rethink the story, tighten loose joists, and added some badly needed shingling to its leaky roof. My sincere thanks to you all.

1

Later, when he thought about what had happened during those months, Luke would always see one big picture—Frankie and the Strike. They were locked together in his memory.

It really hadn't been that way, though. Memory is a picture on paper, without depth. What's missing are the spaces in between.

Luke *was* sure of one thing. It all started the day the miners were kicked out of the company houses. There was a freak September snowstorm that day.

By one-thirty, the parents began arriving to fetch the kids home from school. No one knew what those early snowstorms would do or how long they'd last. Being let out early was a blessing, though, to Luke, like a reprieve.

He and his sister, Beth, got their empty lunch buckets from the cloakroom and ran out into the snow, laughing and feeling free, like on the first day of summer vacation. Pa's Mack truck was waiting for them. It was the biggest vehicle in the school yard. The other parents were grocery and hardware-store merchants and had Model T's or were officers of CFI—Colorado Fuel and Iron—and drove sleek roadsters and touring cars. Pa's big old flatbed chuffed exhaust into the chill air, its body rocking to the motion of its mammoth engine. Empty milk cans were fitted into metal slots Pa had welded onto the bed, and they were rattling like sleigh bells with the rocking motion of the truck. Pa was just coming back from the midday run to the creamery, bringing the empties back home.

Beth and Luke jumped into the cab with him, full of joy, but his face was solemn, like the one he wore during his occasional visits to church.

"They're kicking 'em out of the camps," Pa said. "On a day like this. They've got no conscience."

Luke didn't ask who *they* were as Pa jabbed the truck into gear and fishtailed out of the school yard onto the snow-covered road.

But he soon saw what Pa was talking about. Not two miles from their ranch, at the Walsenburg–Tabasco–Trinidad junction, a long caravan of people was treading along the road, soaked to the skin, with carts and baby buggies and wheelbarrows and all other sorts of wheeled vehicles filled to the brim with boxes and clothes and food.

The Colorado coalfields were made up mostly of company towns. "A feudal kingdom for the Rockefellers," Pa used to say. Red-painted company houses for company employees. Company stores, where the workers had to shop, that sold everything from hairpins to bread for twenty percent higher than regular stores. Company schools that taught the kids just what they'd need to know to be dutiful workers. Even company newspapers and recreation halls. And, worst of all, company spies all over the place, making sure everybody stayed in line, that nobody criticized the system.

If you left your job at CFI, you also left your home. And the miners had just come out on strike, so these homeless strikers and their families walked in silence, looking up at Beth and Luke as their flatbed passed by. Men, women, and kids. Lots of kids all over the place, but they weren't running around crazy like Luke and his friends would do if they were out of school. They just stayed in this long, dark line of people. It seemed everyone was wearing brown or black, and they stood out like fence posts against the whiteness all about.

The snow hadn't let up any, and the people's heads were piled with it. A guy would take off his cap every now and then and slap the snow off, then quick shove it down tight to keep the snow off his hair. The women all wore kerchiefs over their heads.

Pa slowed down to a crawl, giving the people plenty of room on the road. Passing one family, Beth saw a rag doll balanced precariously atop a mound of mattresses and bed linen, and just as they were level with them, the doll fell off.

"Pa!" Beth yelped. "You run over her."

Pa jammed on the brakes. "I didn't see any kid." His eyes were big and scared-looking.

Beth hopped out of the cab, peering under the wheels. "Pull ahead, Pa. You're still on it."

"A doll," Luke said.

Pa sighed and rubbed the bridge of his nose like he did when he couldn't find one of the cows at night, and he let out the clutch to ease forward. Beth had retrieved the rag doll, and a kid with the little group of people started wailing. Beth held it out to her, but the little girl just cried louder, seeing the doll all crumpled and muddy. One of the men, a big guy with flashing dark eyes and a pirate's black mustache, stepped forward and took the rag doll from Beth's hand, sweeping his wet cap off as he did so and giving her a quick, short bow with his head.

"Sorry," Beth said.

He made a sound like a mix between clearing his throat and saying "Harry's toe."

Pa leaned over Luke to the passenger-side window and nodded at the big man. *"Parakalo,"* he said.

3

This seemed to make all the people a bit happier. Even the bawling kid stopped for a second.

Beth jumped back in the cab, and Pa put the truck in gear again.

"They're Greek," he said, not taking his eyes from the road. "The guy said 'Thanks' and I said 'You're welcome.'"

Beth and Luke looked at each other. A sudden pride swept over Luke that Pa should know another language.

Pa drove on real slow. Finally their turn-off came, just south of Ludlow.

Pa pulled over to the side of the road after they left the thick of the people. He didn't look back at them, just kept his hands on the steering wheel. His knuckles turned white as he gripped harder and harder, and his face took on the same pale color.

Luke craned his neck around and watched the silent, sodden procession.

"But where will they sleep?" Beth said.

Pa said nothing for a moment.

"Pa?" Luke said, beginning to feel worried for those people out there in the snow.

Pa came to himself, letting out air like a punctured bike tire.

"There're supposed to be tents coming for them. But the company boys slowed up the train. They rented land from the Hollearans just above Ludlow. Plan to set up a strikers' camp there."

"In the snow?" Luke said.

Pa made no answer, only put the truck in gear again and plowed through the thick snowfall.

Visibility was bad. They could barely pick out yellow smudges of lights from the ranch. But they couldn't see the twin Spanish Peaks to the west or Fisher's Peak to the

4

southeast. It was just the three of them in a truck in the vast flatland of southern Colorado and the yellow glow in the distance that led them through the snow.

When they finally pulled up in front of the house, Pa put his arm across the seat in back of them.

"Thought I'd tell you. We got us a visitor."

God, please don't let it be Aunt Polly, Luke thought.

"Who is it, Pa?" Beth asked.

"No one you know," he said.

Luke let out a thankful sigh.

"A kid, not much older than you, Luke, by the looks of her. Thirteen, maybe fourteen. Knocked around some, though. Must've fell off the train last night. Lucky she wasn't killed."

Luke looked at his pa, trying to figure out what he wasn't saying.

"Who's she belong to?" Beth asked.

"Far as we can tell, she don't belong to nobody," Pa said. "Seems the fall jarred her head some. Don't remember much."

"Maybe we ought to advertise her in the paper," Luke said.

"Hey, Luke, she's not a heifer or something."

Pa rubbed his head and Beth laughed, but still Luke could sense something unsaid.

"Folks hereabouts know where she is," Pa said. "Word gets out. Somebody lost a kid, they'll know where to come looking."

"She gonna stay here?" Beth said.

Suddenly the new kid didn't seem like such a great thing to Beth, Luke could tell.

Pa just shrugged. "We'll wait and see."

Luke jumped out of the cab, and his feet sank a good six inches into the snow.

"Get your work clothes on," Pa ordered as Luke clumped up the front steps. "Got to get the cows in for the night."

But he didn't head for his room straight off. He wanted to see this kid for himself. Inside, it was cozy and warm, with the sweet smell of baking bread. Ma sat in the rocker by the stove, her back to them, and as they approached, she half turned and put a finger to her lips to shush them.

Coming alongside the chair, they could see that there was a kid with Ma, sleeping curled up like a lapdog, her head resting against Ma's chest, her long legs draped over the arms of the rocker. The kid's blond hair was cut short and raggedy like a boy's, but her skin wasn't boylike at all. It was soft-looking and white like marble. Her nose was tiny and sharp, and she had lips red like cherry cough drops. At her right temple a blue vein pulsed in rhythm to her breathing.

Looking at the two of them there in that rocker, Luke felt a nudging little pain in the pit of his stomach. Partly it was the girl, so fragile-looking, so trusting. And partly it was Ma. Ever since his brother, Tom, died last year, she'd been like some machine, going through the motions, cooking and washing and keeping the house clean, but not so much as a hug or a pat on the head for him or Beth. Luke looked down at Ma now, smiling as she cradled this runaway in her lap.

"Her name's Francine," Ma whispered. "She's starting to remember things."

Pa tapped Luke's shoulder, whispering in his ear, "Let's get them cows in before their udders freeze and we're stuck with fifty gallons of ice cream."

At dinner, washed up and feeling dog tired after trudging through snow and mud to find all the cows, Luke ate in silence. Not so Francine, who was suddenly making a miraculous recovery.

". . . and after my parents died," she was saying, "I stayed with my aunt and uncle in upstate New York."

She pronounced *aunt* like it was spelled with an *ah*, like the actors who would come to Trinidad once a year and put on plays in the Grange Hall, Luke thought.

Ma just smiled at her. Beth caught Luke's eye, crossed hers, and went back to eating.

"But what made you run away, dear?" Ma asked.

Francine sat up straight in her chair, dressed in an oversized pinafore that Ma used to wear in her slimmer days. That vein in her temple throbbed in time to his own heart beat, fascinating Luke. She was so pretty despite her chopped-off hair and so self-assured. But there was something phony to her, Luke thought. Just like those actors who came to town.

"They died, too," she said, her face suddenly clouding. "Everyone I ever love dies. I think I'm cursed."

Thinking of those actors made her words all the more familiar. Luke sat up in his chair now, squinting at her. He had actually seen the play she was doing; he was sure of it. Two springs ago. Ma had sat through it, too, but here she was, soaking this all in like it was the first time she ever heard it. He told himself the next line: "And rather than the poorhouse, I ran away to seek my fortune."

"And rather than being sent to the poorhouse," Francine said right on cue, "I ran away to seek my fortune. I cut my hair and acted like I was a boy."

Luke smiled, a wide, easy grin. Miss Francine Prancine, I've got you. And he thrust a hunk of fried pork chop into his mouth at the thought.

Later, after Francine went up to bed in Tom's room, Luke tried to talk to Ma about the traveling theater company, but she just glared at him.

"Don't you have some homework to do?" was all she would say. But he was sure Ma remembered the play. He

7

could see the little glimmer of recognition in her eyes when he mentioned it. So how come she was letting Francine get away with the lies? What did she know that she wasn't telling?

Luke didn't sleep well that night. First he thought of Francine, wondering what her real story was and how long she'd be staying at the ranch. Pa and Ma had taken in stray animals before, but never a stray kid. He was beginning to wish it had been Aunt Polly come to visit—at least she had a home to go back to. But there wasn't much point in thinking about that. It was something for Ma and Pa to decide.

Then he conjured up a vision of all those miners and their families out in the cold in Ludlow, wondering if their tents and blankets ever got there. He didn't know much about strikes or the mines, only that his brother, Tom, had been killed in the number-three shaft at Primero, working to earn some money to go to college. Instead, they brought him and sixty-five others out in wooden boxes after an explosion.

"Too cheap to water down the dust," Pa kept saying after the tragedy. "For the few dollars it would've cost to lay water on the coal dust, they kill sixty-six good men and boys. Miserable damned capitalists."

At which point Ma usually hushed Pa. But he returned the seventy-five dollars CFI sent for burying money.

"Blood money," he'd hissed as he ripped up the check and stuffed the pieces in an envelope to send back.

Luke couldn't take his mind off the crunched-up rag doll from this afternoon or the man with the flashing eyes or the little girl who was crying so hard over the doll. None of the mine kids went to his school, so he didn't have any friends among them. Most of them didn't speak English, anyway.

8

They were from all over, from places with strange names like Serbia, Greece, Austria, Slovenia, Bulgaria, Italy. Luke didn't know much about them, other than the names of their countries. Could hardly even pick those out on a world map, either.

Pa said the miners were only asking to work eight-hour days and six-day weeks, only for their union to be recognized. "Just asking for a little human respect and dignity" was how he put it. Luke didn't see the harm in that.

He tossed and turned and kept thinking how he'd feel out there in the snow tonight. He knew how miserable and scared and lonely he'd be. Like you feel when you hear a train whistle calling in the dead of night.

He rolled over in his bed once more, the springs creaking, and heard a funny sound coming from Tom's room. At first it sounded like a mournful old train whistle. Then he listened real hard and finally made it out: little sobs in the night, when Francine figured all of them were asleep.

2

The shooting started two days later. They could hear it from up the draw toward evening. Snow had let up and the sun was out again, glowing pink on Fisher's Peak. There were three short, sharp cracks followed by a small explosion like the sound Pa's twelve-gauge made pheasant hunting.

Ma bustled onto the porch, Francine behind her.

"You hear that?" she said.

Beth and Luke had given up on the snowman they'd been trying to keep from melting for the past day.

"Sounds like gunshots," Luke said.

"You kids get in here right now," Ma hollered. "Where's your pa?"

"In the barn," Luke said, wondering how she could not know the milking schedule after all these years.

Pa poked his head out of the barn just then. "Those shots?"

Luke nodded to him. The light was growing fainter. The rosy hue on Fisher's Peak was all but gone, and the evening star shone overhead. There was a smell like a mixture of cow dung and fresh water. A smell like the spring: snow melting in September.

"Better go take a look-see," Pa said.

Beth and Luke stopped in their tracks midway to the porch.

"You'll do no such thing, Jethro," Ma said, clutching Francine to her apron.

Pa sidled over and winked. "Coming with me, Luke?"

Ma was still upbraiding them from the porch, and Beth was crying about how it was unfair she couldn't go as Pa and Luke hopped into the flatbed. They started her up and jostled down the pitted road in the general direction of the shots. Suddenly, Ma started yelling at them real loud, but they didn't pay her any attention. There'd be trouble enough later on, though, Luke knew.

Soon they were following the course of the Purgatoire—the little creek known locally as the Picketwire—and headed toward the coking plants at Segundo. It was strange not to see the smudge of black cloud announcing those plants. Shut down. There was no activity in Segundo itself. But just outside of town, near a little footbridge over the Picketwire, they saw a white horse without a rider and a group of men all looking down at the ground on the far side of the creek.

Luke knew what was up before he even got out of the cab. It was the horse, Marshal Bob Lee's horse. Everybody in Las Animas and Huerfano counties knew that white stallion standing thirteen hands high.

Pa and Luke got out at the same time, and Luke headed around the front of the truck to where the horse stood. It was snorting steam into the chill air, stomping the ground with its right forehoof, and gazing wild-eyed at all the commotion.

"Well I'll be," Pa said in back of him. "Get on down from there, you little minx."

Luke looked back and saw Pa handing Francine down off the bed of the truck. So that's what Ma was yelling at, he thought. Francine must've jumped on as they were bumping down the drive away from the barn. But he had no time to wonder why she had come, for at that very moment, the sheriff's black sedan came racing up the draw, throwing mud behind it.

Luke went to the horse and took its reins in hand.

"Easy, fella," he said. But Lee's horse wasn't going to be easy at all. It reared its head back, then made a lunge at Luke's hand with its teeth bared. As ornery as its owner, he told himself, dropping its reins. "Heck with you then," he said. "Go get yourself lost if you want to." The horse trotted off to a patch of grass showing through the melting snow. Luke noticed that Lee's rifle scabbard at the side of the saddle was empty.

Sheriff Farr's car pulled to a halt and doors opened and then slammed shut.

"The hell's going on here?" Sheriff Farr growled at no one in particular. Luke took his eyes off the horse and looked at the group of men. Pa and Francine were standing hand in hand several yards apart from them. Luke was on the other side, and the light was going all pearly over the Spanish Peaks to the west and making the snow look washed-out purple after sunset.

"They shot him, Sheriff," said one of the men, a guard at the mine dressed in a blue woolen CFI uniform.

"Anybody see who done it?" Farr, a massive man whose clothes seemed always to be too small for him, shouldered his way into the crowd. As they made way for him, the body lying at the men's feet became visible to Luke. There was a big, raggedy hole in Lee's neck, and blood was pooling out onto the muddy snow.

The sheriff took his Stetson off, ran a hand through his red hair. "Somebody's gonna pay for this."

Luke wasn't sorry to see Bob Lee stretched out there. He knew it was a terrible thing to think, but the man was a bully and a crook who just happened to wear a badge. Word was he'd been some kind of outlaw himself before being recruited out of New Mexico to serve in the sheriff's department. He'd shot a Greek kid the summer before for stealing a handful of coal from the company stocks. Said as how the kid was armed and dangerous, but all the guy had in his hands when they carted the body away to Potter's Field was a bunch of coal. And Lee was also the sort on market days in Trinidad, to give mothers that certain kind of look, that made them want to go straight home and wash, or the kind who shoved kids out of the way on the town's sidewalks. Still, Luke figured he shouldn't have been happy to see him sprawled out there, dead from a shotgun wound to the neck.

"Bunch of them Greeks done it," the guard said. "Trying to steal back onto company property."

"Maybe they were just trying to get some of their possessions out of their former houses," Pa said. This made the other men turn toward him for the first time. Sheriff Farr looked Pa up and down like he was measuring him for prison clothes, and then he took in Francine, too.

"And maybe you shouldn't ought to stick your nose in where it don't belong, Hayes."

Pa stiffened at this remark but didn't say any more.

"Poor old Bob here," the guard went on. "He was chasing three of them over the bridge when some coward shot him from ambush."

Lee's carbine lay not far from his body. Luke remembered the three sharp cracks coming before the shotgun blast. No doubt in his mind who'd fired first. He could just see Lee trying to run the men down, shooting at their backs as they scattered in terror.

"Greeks, huh?" Sheriff Farr said, not taking his eyes off the corpse. It was like he was fascinated by death, wanted to get a mental picture of it to carry around with him and take out occasionally to build up his anger and hate.

The men were so consumed by looking at Lee's corpse

13

that they did not at first notice a young man walking down the road toward the CFI camp entrance. He wore blue dungarees and a matching jacket with a red bandanna at his neck. A miner for sure, and a striker, too, Luke figured, by the color of the neck scarf. A redneck.

Lee's horse neighed, and another one of the mine guards looked up from the body and noticed the striker, who seemed completely unaware of the tragedy just played out here, as well as of the danger he was in.

"There goes one of them rednecks now," the guard, a thin, cadaverous-looking man, yelled out. "Get him, boys!"

The miner heard this but looked in back of him as the guard pointed his way, as if he could not imagine being the object of anybody's interest. He didn't even run as the guards and two others went for him. They grabbed him by the arms and pulled him back to Farr. Not much of a job because the miner wasn't resisting. Luke edged around the men to stand next to Pa and Francine. She looked at him with hooded eyes, gripping Pa's hand tight.

"Well, what we got here?" Sheriff Farr said as the Greek was pushed in front of him.

He was a real young guy. There was barely even fuzz on his upper lip. He looked around at the men with eyes as big and scared as those of Lee's stallion.

"Come on," Farr shouted into his face. "Speak up. What you doing here?"

The kid still didn't say anything, half frightened out of his wits.

Sheriff Farr's meaty fist suddenly landed square in the middle of his face, crushing his nose, spraying blood on one of the guards, and lifting the kid off his feet to lay him out flat on his back in the snow.

"Hold on, Sheriff," Pa said, dropping Francine's hand

and moving toward the men. "The kid probably can't speak English."

"He's one of 'em, for sure," the first guard said, bending over the immobile body and staring into the young miner's face.

"Hang the coward," someone else said in the group of men.

"What's he doing coming back here if he was in on it?" Pa said. "Nobody's gonna be that dumb."

Sheriff Farr swung around on Pa now, his hand resting on the grip of his holstered .45.

"I told you to butt out, Hayes. Unless you want to join this foreigner in jail, that is."

Pa stood his ground facing Sheriff Farr, and Luke suddenly got so scared his stomach cramped, more scared than he'd ever been in his life before. It was like he could smell the danger in the air, could see Pa going for the sheriff's throat and see the sheriff drawing his gun. They'd been distant enemies for years, Pa saying Farr was in the pay of the Rockefellers and CFI. But now it was a lot more than just talk. There was a sour taste in the back of Luke's throat. He wanted to leave. Now.

But Pa continued to stand his ground. The sheriff glared at him.

Francine started to moan, holding her stomach.

"Oh, Uncle Jethro, please! Get me home. I'm terrible sick."

No fancy accent to her voice now. She sounded like some local kid, twang and all. Luke stared at her in amazement.

"I'm about to burst, Uncle. Get me home."

Pa turned around, his face looking as surprised as Luke's.

"That's right, Hayes," the sheriff said. "Get the child home. You got no business bringing a little girl into this."

Francine folded into Pa's arms like a falling leaf, and he carried her back to the cab of the truck. Luke followed, and they all got in. The young miner was still sprawled on the ground near Lee's body.

Pa called out to the men from his open window. "I'm a witness here, Sheriff. That kid better get a fair trial."

At which Francine yelped out louder than ever, and Pa started up the truck and headed back home.

Not a hundred yards from the scene, Francine sat up straight in the seat between them and glanced back at the sheriff and the other men.

"Thought you was sick, Francine," Pa said.

She looked ahead now and waited a few moments before speaking.

"That pea-brain cop was gonna drill you a new belly button in a second or so. It was the only thing I could think of doing."

Not a blink. Not as much as a peek from the corner of her eye at either of them. Pa and Luke exchanged glances, and nothing more was said until they got home. Ma read both Pa and Luke the riot act for "enticing little Francine" away with them, giving them no chance to say word one. Meanwhile, Francine once again became the meek little romancer from upstate New York, not the street-smart urchin she sounded like when talking about Pa's new belly button.

Later that night, after everybody else was asleep, Luke got up and knocked on Tom's door. No sobs from inside tonight, but when he opened it, he could see she was still awake, too, sitting on the window seat and looking at the moon high over the prairie. She didn't bother to look around as he entered. He'd intended to tell her off tonight, to let her know that he saw through her, that he knew what she was up to. He was even going to tell her the name of the play she stole her lines from. But the incident with Sheriff Farr changed all that.

"I just wanted to say thanks," Luke said. "That whole business this evening could've gone wrong."

She nodded, not taking her eyes off the moon.

Finally she said, "There's an owl out there. I don't think I've ever seen one outside a zoo before."

The way she ignored his thanks made him suddenly want to tell her that he knew her secret, at least part of it. That she might be able to string his parents along with her lies, but not him. But that he wasn't going to say anything for the time being.

"What'll they do to him?" she asked before he could get such a declaration out. She turned to look at him, and the moonlight on her profile exactly matched the shade of her hair and made her look like an angel.

"Put him on trial, I guess. He didn't do it. Pa was right. He'd never have come back if he did."

She shrugged. "They're all so stupid."

Luke misunderstood. "Right. And that's why the miners are striking. Because of that kind of stupidity."

He wanted to impress her with his fervor, with his commitment to what was right, but she only laughed at him.

"No," she said. "I mean the strikers. They're dumb as a table if they think they can beat the bosses. The owners always win. Don't they know that?"

"But all they're asking for is some dignity," he said, repeating Pa's words.

"Oh, lovely," she said, turning again to the window. "That and a nickel will get you a haircut in New York. The kid's a dead man. They're all dead unless they get as many guns as the bosses."

There was a cold, hard knowing in her voice that Luke

could not match or argue with. But as he was leaving, she offered one more piece of information.

"By the way, they call me Frankie."

Luke went back to bed and slept poorly.

Next day they heard that the Greek kid had been shot dead while trying to escape from custody. Pa went to town to give his information, to make some protest, with Ma following him all the way out to the truck, telling him not to do it, that it wasn't his business. But Pa just clenched his jaw tight and went to town. He came back in the late afternoon looking tired and bewildered, like he'd lost something.

"They had witnesses, Anne," he said to Ma once he'd sat down in the kitchen with a cup of coffee to warm him. "Three of them to say the young boy was violent and tried to run away." He gulped the coffee, and Luke watched it all from the doorway, not invited in, not shooed away.

"Witnesses," Pa said again, but this time like it was cussing.

3

Monday of the next week Frankie was sent to school with Beth and Luke.

"You watch out for her, Luke. Hear?" Ma said as they were leaving.

"Sure."

"Hear?"

"Okay." He avoided her eyes, knowing they would be fixed on him like headlights.

Pa sat in the Mack, its exhaust blowing into the brisk fall morning. Cows were out in the south pasture munching away peaceful as could be. No school for them. Luke thought maybe he'd like to be a cow next life.

It was tight in the cab with all four of them. Frankie sat next to Pa, which didn't please Beth much. Luke got the door. Riding shotgun, they called it. That didn't please Beth even more.

She wrinkled up her face. "When do I get to sit next to the door, Pa?"

"You kids'll trade off," he said.

"Well, it's not fair," she whined.

Frankie sat in silence, her chopped-off hair covered in one of Ma's kerchiefs so that she looked like one of the kids from the strikers' camp. Luke stole little glances at her out of the corner of his eye.

Out at the main road, Pa turned left, headed north, the opposite direction of the school.

"Where we going, Pa?" Luke asked.

He didn't respond at first, just started whistling a sort of hymn song he liked. "Stopping by the camp to deliver something," he said.

Luke felt his heart race. He hadn't been to the camp at Ludlow since they put all the tents up. And maybe they'd get so busy there they'd have to miss some school. He felt Beth wiggle next to him with the same sort of anticipation.

The tents were visible from a long way off. They sat in the little bowl at Ludlow just to the north of the small town, a whole army of white canvas pitched in regular lines. Blocks and blocks of them in the bare plain. The Stars and Stripes whipped in the wind at the entrance, and as they got closer, it looked like there was a fair going on. Kids were running around the tents, calling out and yelping to one another. Fresh wash hung out on the lines, flapping in the breeze like flags. Men and women stood in front of their tents, smiling and yabbering away in foreign tongues like it was some kind of festival or something.

"Why do they look so happy, Pa?" Beth asked as he pulled the truck to a stop in front of the tent colony. The Mack kept running for a while after Pa turned it off and rattled to a stop finally.

Pa looked from the girls to Luke. "They're happy 'cause they're finally standing up for themselves."

With that, he swung out of the cab. "You kids wait here. I'll be right back." But on second thought, he said, "You come with me, Luke. You can help with the cans."

"Not fair," Beth was whining, but Luke paid no attention, scrambling down from the cab as fast as he could.

Pa went up and started talking to a little woman with the reddest hair Luke had ever seen. When she smiled, it was like the sun was shining. She laughed at something Pa was saying, and even her laugh sounded like music.

20

"And this here's my son, Luke," he said as the boy walked up to them.

She held out her hand, a dainty little thing. "I'm Mary Thomas," she said, and there was a peculiar kind of lilt to her voice. Not Irish, not Scottish. They shook hands, and her little mitt caught him by surprise, giving his hand the kind of shake that pops a couple of knuckles.

"Pleased to meet you, ma'am," Luke said as soon as he retrieved his bruised paw.

"Where do you want the cans, Mrs. Thomas?" Pa asked.

"Mary, please. And they'll do nicely over here."

She nodded toward a huge tent dead in the middle of all the others, sort of an all-purpose meeting and dining hall. Not that they needed a separate dining hall, for all the individual tents were outfitted with a stove, wooden floors, half walls, and plenty of furniture. Luke got a peek in Mrs. Thomas's tent as they were hauling milk cans from the truck, and it was like somebody's fancy parlor, with a lace tablecloth on the table, curtains on the little windows, and feather beds. He also caught sight of Frankie wandering around, rubbernecking at everything. She should have been back in the truck with Beth, but Luke wasn't about to say anything. Pa could catch her at it himself.

They set the cans down next to a center table, which had a pitcher and a row of porcelain mugs on it. Luke was just going out of the tent when he saw a kid, maybe a couple years younger than himself, staring at the milk cans. He caught Luke's glance and started to walk away. His washed-out dungarees looked about four sizes too big for him, rolled up around skinny ankles, and his feet were bare. Saving the boots for winter, Luke figured.

"Hey," Luke called to him. "It's okay. We brought it for you people."

The kid turned, peering at Luke closely.

21

"You with the Company?"

Luke half laughed. "Heck, no. Pa, he runs a dairy over yonder." Luke nodded vaguely in the direction of their ranch.

The kid's eyes widened at this information. "You mean you get milk like this all the time?"

By now he'd made his way to the trestle table and was looking over the rim of one of the milk cans into its contents.

"Go on," Luke said, "It's for drinking."

The kid didn't wait to be asked twice, but dipped one of the pitchers in and brought it out dripping. He poured himself a good big mug of it and swallowed it in one gulp. There was white from his lip to his nose, and he wiped at it with his sleeve.

He was a funny-looking kid, Luke thought, skinny as a rabbit and about as twitchy.

"I'm Luke." But the kid just stared at the pitcher of milk. "Well, go on. But don't make yourself sick."

The kid poured a smaller helping and took his time, swallowing it in two gulps instead of one.

"You go to school or something?" Luke asked.

"We're strikers."

"Yeah. But what do you do all day?"

"Strike."

Luke figured the kid's marble bag wasn't quite full, and then the kid said, "Beats learning the math tables, don't it?" He shot a grin at Luke, looking like some sort of elf.

A woman's voice sounded from nearby. "Frank! Frank Snyder! Where are you, boy? I need your help."

The kid's ears pricked up at the sound of the voice.

"That's my ma," he said. "That's my name, too. Nice meeting you, Luke."

And he was off, like a rabbit through the brush. Luke

thought it was a pretty good coincidence, the name and all. Frank and Frankie.

Back at the truck, Mrs. Thomas was trying to give Pa some cash for the milk, but he just looked at her level, like he did when a cow wouldn't give milk, and shook his head.

"I'm not doing this for money, Mrs. Thomas."

"Now don't be silly. And please call me Mary." She made to stuff the bills in his shirt pocket.

"Don't you be silly, Mary," Pa said, moving her hand away. "I had an older son die in these mines. I sort of have him in mind when I bring this milk. You'd be doing me a favor to take it, if you understand."

Mrs. Thomas nodded her head, looking at Pa with eyes as gray as a thunderhead. She crinkled up her nose some then. "I do understand. We lost a good number of our boys in the Welsh mines, too. It's like a fraternity. A fraternity of lost souls."

Pa grinned. "So, I'll be seeing you tomorrow."

"That'd be fine." She smiled at Luke now. "Nice meeting you, Luke. You'll be helping your dad?"

"Sure."

"Well, then, I'll be seeing you, too."

He felt his chest expanding a couple of inches with her smile. By God, he'd carry the cans all by himself tomorrow, not him on one side and Pa on the other, stumbling along like today.

They stood at the truck for a moment before getting in. He noticed Frankie had beat them back and was sitting next to the steering wheel, looking bored.

Gazing around the camp, Luke decided he liked it here—liked the fresh smell of the air away from the cows and barn at their own place. He liked the activity, the hustle and bustle of a miniature city of twelve hundred people. And he liked Mrs. Thomas.

23

Luke saw Pa was admiring her, too, humming to himself, but his song was cut short by the piercing whistle of a train approaching. The camp had been built close to the tracks of the Colorado and Southern Railroad, and now you could see why. The train made a clickety-clack racket as it crossed the steel bridge just north of the camp, and by the sound of it, she was a long, old train. As it came into sight, men from the camp began lining the tracks. Suddenly the festive air was gone, and the strikers began shouting at the train, raising their fists at it. Some of them even threw a piece of coal or a rock.

The train was chockablock full of men. They were packed in the open cars like soldiers off to war. At first they stared with amazement, waving at the men along the tracks, yelling out in all sorts of foreign tongues. They were smiling; it was a lark. But then they saw that the men along the tracks were waving their fists at them. A chunk of coal struck a little fat guy on one of the cars, hit him on the shoulder, and then the faces that rattled by lost their smiles. There was fear that turned to anger in their faces. Luke looked at Pa, not understanding what this was all about.

"Scabs," he hissed. "They're bringing 'em in from out of state."

The word sounded mean in Luke's ears. Scab was something you called somebody if you wanted to fight. Something you called somebody when every other dirty word failed.

The train hooted past the Ludlow depot, not even slowing. It curled to the right just under Water Tank Hill, and after a few minutes, the last of the cars was lost in the bare hills and pinyon pines. But the men kept standing along the tracks, silent now, just staring at the metal rails like they were twin snakes bringing poison into their lives.

*   *   *

Pa dropped them off at school without ceremony. He was eager to get on with the morning milk run into Trinidad. Luke wished he could be with him, but instead, here he was, walking up the sodden path to the one-room schoolhouse with all the guys looking at Frankie wearing Ma's kerchief.

She just kept her head up, though, and walked right into the school without even batting an eye at the boys ogling her. Beth went off to her group of girlfriends, and Luke ended up following Frankie into the schoolhouse so as he could introduce her to Miss Nielson, their teacher.

Miss Nielson was busy shoveling coal into the potbellied stove. It was already glowing and the room was stuffy with the heat, but Miss Nielson, a tall and reedy young woman fresh out of teachers' college, liked to stoke that stove till it got humming. She was from down in southern New Mexico, and it was warmer there. She was bundled up in a couple layers of baggy cardigans over her plain blue dress, and she shoveled like it was a penance.

"Miss Nielson," Luke said to her back. "Ma said I was to bring Francine here to school."

Frankie shot him a squint-eyed look at the use of that name, but Ma had told him to use it.

Miss Nielson turned around, her cheeks all red from the exertion and the heat. You couldn't call her a pretty woman. In fact, you could hardly call her a woman at all, for she was not much older than Samuel Kincaid, the oldest boy in school and the son of a Trinidad shopkeeper. Most of the boys when they turned sixteen were already down in the mines, but not Samuel. He was headed for college, and he never got tired of telling all the other kids that fact. Miss Nielson wore glasses, and they had slipped

25

down her nose some. She jabbed them up with a forefinger and smiled at Frankie.

"That's very nice," she said, but without much enthusiasm. "We can always use another bright pupil."

"My name's Frankie."

"I'm sure it is," Miss Nielson said. "And mine's Miss Nielson. What grade are you in, Frankie?"

It was like she asked what the capital of Austria–Hungary was. Frankie just stared at Miss Nielson, and a muscle played in her cheek. It was the first time Luke had seen her at a loss for words.

"Where did you go to school before?" Miss Nielson asked.

"She's from New York City," Luke blurted out.

"That is a long way away." Miss Nielson put down the shovel into the coal scuttle. Frankie said nothing.

"Why don't you go fill up the scuttle, Luke, while Frankie and I get to know each other."

It was half full already, but he didn't protest. The coal pile was out back of the schoolhouse, a mound of the black stuff, which Billy Wilder's dad replenished regularly from the CFI supplies. He was glad enough to let Frankie and Miss Nielson figure it out from here.

He took his time with the coal, and then the bell started ringing and the kids all headed into the school. Luke put the scuttle down by the stove and then joined Phil and Peter at their bench.

"Who's she?" Phil asked, nodding at Frankie as she took a seat on the girls' side of the room.

"She's visiting," Luke said. He pulled his slate out of the shelf built under the bench. "From New York."

"New York." Peter said it like a foreign word. He was a fat kid, so big in the belly that he had to sit back from the table several inches. As a result, Phil and Luke—who shared the bench with him—were always having to hunch over the table to get at their work.

"Yeah," Luke said. "New York. It's a city in the East."

"I know where it is," Peter said. He pulled a couple of crumbs of bread out of his pants pocket and munched on them with his hand covering his mouth so Miss Nielson wouldn't see. It was against the rules to eat during class time.

"What's she doing here?" he said.

Luke shrugged, saying nothing.

"She a relative?" Phil asked.

Miss Nielson saved him from further questioning by starting the morning prayer and then the flag salute. While they were all standing, he noticed that Frankie wasn't saying the words with them. She just looked stone cold at the limp flag hanging from its pole next to a picture of President Wilson and clapped her right hand to her chest, but didn't say word one.

Then they all sat down and got to work. There was no talking allowed. Miss Nielson had the lesson plans laid out for them each week. Luke's was lying on the table in front of them: thirty-eight to fifty-seven in the math book; fifteen pages of world geography; and for English, a story to read about some old buzzard who goes to Alaska for the gold and dies instead. Uplifting stuff, but they needed to write a report on it to read in front of the class for Friday. Miss Nielson would stop at their desk a couple of times during the day to make sure they were working and to help out if anybody was having problems. There were no problems for the three of them. Luke, Peter, and Phil had it all worked out. Phil was a whiz at math, Peter did okay with geography, and Luke, well, his specialty was English. He was the kind of kid who got a kick out of reading a package of oatmeal.

As they plugged along, Luke caught a glimpse of Frankie now and then. Seemed she was working with the little kids, so he figured Miss Nielson had her helping out. Maybe she'd already gone way beyond anything they were doing in their little school. Coming from New York, what could she learn in a little one-roomer on the Colorado prairie?

4

But things got clearer at first recess. Beth came up to him where he was playing marbles with the guys.

"Hey, Luke," she said, tugging at his sweater just as he was shooting. This made him miss Billy Wilder's agate shooter. He'd been wanting that for months, ever since Billy brought it back with him from a vacation in San Francisco. He'd dreamt about it and schemed how to get Billy into just the right game. He had a chance, and now he'd gone and blown it. And there was his favorite shooter lying within shooting distance of Billy's agate.

"What do you want?" Luke said, swinging around on her, his face getting red with anger. "You should be over with the girls."

Billy Wilder took careful aim and blistered Luke's marble, taking a chunk out of it so that he wasn't even interested in keeping it.

"Thanks a lot, midget," Luke said to Beth after pocketing his damaged shooter.

"But it's important. It's about Francine Smancine."

"So. What about her?"

Beth squared her little shoulders and grinned. "She can't read."

"What?"

"You hard of hearing? I said she can't read."

"But Miss Nielson has her working with the little kids."

" 'Cause she can't read. She's doing the same work as the first graders."

This sent Beth into a giggle spasm that made her lose her breath and start coughing.

"Get back to the other girls," Luke said.

"Isn't it great? Fancy Smancy can't even read."

But he didn't feel like rejoicing. No wonder Frankie hadn't been any too eager to go to school with them.

The real trouble started at afternoon recess. Some of the guys were hanging around the swings and parallel bars. Betty Carlson liked to spin on the bars, liked it way too much because it was the only thing she could do well. She wasn't really simple, but she was pretty close to it. And the guys liked to be there for the performance. Sometimes they got to see all of her thigh and underwear when her skirts flew over her head. Billy Wilder was usually in the front row, cheering Betty on, telling her how great she was on the bar.

"Do it again, Betty!" he'd yell. "You're better than the trapeze artists in the circus."

He was laughing at her all the time, but she took encouragement from it. Nobody ever gave her much otherwise.

Usually this never lasted very long. The bell would ring or Miss Nielson would come out on the playground and then all the boys would scatter. But today it seemed to go on forever and ever.

"One more time," Billy yelled, and Betty smiled sort of dizzy-like and spun around and her skirts blew out in the wind and there were her undies, all gray and tattered. Luke was out of the marble game with a lame shooter, and he watched the guys egging her on, thinking he ought to do something to stop it, when suddenly Frankie marched up to Billy Wilder.

"Why don't *you* go spin around that bar if you like it so much."

Billy blinked at her like he didn't believe she'd just said that. The girls stuck to themselves during recess, and besides, nobody ever talked to Billy Wilder like that. Not even his dad.

"What's it to you?" he finally blurted out.

"I don't like what you're doing. That's what it is to me."

Billy Wilder tried to stare her down, and the guys around him were waiting for a put-down that would send this newcomer on her way. Luke took his hands out of his pockets and started over to them.

Betty stopped spinning and looked at the group gathered around Frankie.

"What's the matter?" she said. "Don't you like my trapeze act anymore?"

But nobody was paying any attention to her. All eyes were on Frankie and Billy.

"You've got a lot of nerve coming in here telling us how to act," Billy said. "Why, you're nothing but a . . . a . . . ."

Luke hoped he wouldn't say it. He tried to get to them before Billy could utter the word.

". . . but a *scab*," Billy said.

A tense silence came over the other guys. They knew what it meant. But Frankie just stood there in her kerchief and Ma's old gray coat, shaking her head at him, having no idea of the challenge just thrown at her.

Finally she stuck her chin out at him and said, "And you're nothing but a little piece of dog crap that people step on in the street."

Billy took it like he'd just been hit. It was even more quiet then. Kids from all over the playground began to

31

congregate by the parallel bars. Beth and her friends were at the outer reaches of the crowd gathered around Frankie and Billy, and they started singing:

> *"Billy and Frankie sittin' in a tree,*
> *K-I-S-S-I-N-G."*

"Shut up, Beth," Luke said as he moved into the crowd. Janey Jones, Beth's best friend, stuck her tongue out at Luke, but he let it go.

"Oh yeah?" Billy Wilder was saying as Luke pushed his way to the middle.

Next step in the escalation would be the first shove, Luke knew. Samuel Kincaid was edging around Frankie to kneel down in back of her so Billy could shove her over him. Luke went up behind Frankie, cutting Samuel off.

"What's going on?" he said.

Frankie didn't twitch a muscle. She kept her eyes locked on Billy's. Billy quick looked at Luke and then back to Frankie. Luke could tell he didn't know quite what to do. His mouth had got him into a fix. He'd made the fight by calling her a scab, but he still wasn't sure if it was okay to hit a girl.

"This little scab belong to you, Hayes?"

"I don't belong to anybody," she shot back.

"Maybe we should just talk about this," Luke said.

Billy's eyes—mean little piggy eyes, too close together—tracked back to Luke. Billy was about a head taller and one year older. Luke had never given much thought to whether Billy could fight or not. Company kids didn't do much fighting. He was soft, but he had both weight and height on Luke. So Luke spent a moment checking him up and down for a weak spot. Pa always said the other guy would have a weak spot. Feet too close together, hands held too low or too high. A temper too fiery so that the guy would swing wild and want to end it too quick. There's always a weak spot. Billy looked like he had them all.

"What's there to talk about? She comes butting in here where she doesn't belong. What's to talk about?"

Luke tried to get between Billy and Frankie, but she wasn't having any of it. Her sharp elbow dug into his side.

"Come on," Luke said. "Let's get back to the marbles. I got a steely here." He tapped his pocket where only his beat-up shooter lay.

"What's with you, Hayes?" Billy said, turning his anger onto Luke now. Simpler for him that way. "She your girl-friend or something? A scab girlfriend?"

Simpler for Luke, too, like this. He pushed Frankie out of the way and jabbed at Billy with his left, then punched him in the gut with his right. Luke heard the wind go out of him, watched his face go red and his eyes bulge.

A hand grabbed Luke from the back and whirled him around.

"Not very nice, Hayes."

He watched stupidly as Samuel Kincaid's fist came flying into his face. The punch seemed to take forever to land, but he couldn't do anything to get out of its way. There was a flashing light and pretty good pain; then he tasted warm, salty blood in the back of his throat. Samuel almost knocked Luke down with the punch, and as he was stum-bling, trying to get a stance, Billy Wilder tackled him from the side and climbed on top, pinning Luke's hands down with his knees. The kids were all yelling and hooting, and Billy had a pretty good time with Luke's face before Miss Nielson came along and pulled him off.

Nobody would tell her what the fight was about, and she shooed them all back into the classroom early.

"I'll be talking to your parents" is all she said to Billy and Luke.

Betty Carlson came up to Frankie as they were going in.

"Thanks a lot," she said. But she didn't mean it. "You spoiled it all. They were liking me. Why don't you just mind your own business, you scab."

Frankie didn't look at Luke as they filed into the school, and Miss Nielson had to yell a few times to get some order before everyone would shut up about the fight and stop replaying it to one another. Luke sat quiet the rest of the day, not feeling much like reading about some old geezer pegging out in Alaska, not feeling even like finishing the chocolate chip cookie Ma had packed in his lunch. He gave it to Peter instead.

When the class was over and they were getting ready to leave, Frankie finally came up to him. Luke smiled sheepishly at her. The white knight.

Before he could say anything, she blurted right out, "I don't want your help. Understand?" She glared at him like he was the one who called her a scab. "I fight my own fights. And I do it a whole lot better than you."

She stomped off into the school yard, looking for Pa's truck.

That night Luke went to bed without supper. Ma didn't believe in strapping kids, but Pa, after listening to Miss Nielson, had been highly in favor of it. They both asked what the fight was about, but Luke kept silent, daring Beth with fierce eyes to say anything. It would have been like trying to buy his way out of it to explain, and he wasn't in the mood. He wasn't in the mood for much of anything, feeling confused and betrayed. He'd only been trying to help, and Frankie made him feel like some kind of idiot for doing so.

34

It must have been about eleven when there was a light tap at his door. He didn't do anything at first, then got up slowly and went to the door. Nobody there. On the landing was a biscuit from supper. Nobody in the hall, no sound from downstairs. There was a light from under Tom's door, though. It flickered, then went out.

5

"Maybe we could steal some of Ma's pretty combs and put them in her room," Beth said later that same week. "Make out like Francine stole them."

Beth and Luke were out in the milk barn, skimming off the cream. Steam was rising from the cows in their stalls and Pokey and Petunia, the two barn cats, were rubbing around their legs, hoping there'd be some spills for them. You could never tell which was Pokey and which Petunia. They were identical tortoise-shell cats, even down to the funny yellow left eye. Beth claimed she knew them apart, but then she claimed lots of things.

"What do you think?" she said, dipping her finger into the pail and holding it out to the cats to lick.

Luke didn't look at her, intent on ladling. "I think maybe you'll make a pretty good criminal."

"We've got to do something."

There was enough whine in her voice to send a shiver up his spine, but he kept on ladling the thick cream into the wooden trough for cheese making. He liked this time of day: last light and the barn all mysterious-looking. You couldn't see into any of the corners, but there would be rapid movement once in a while, and then one of the cats would set out on a chase. The cows huffed and stomped a hoof now and again, and the place smelled rich of hay and animal. Luke was feeling just fine. The bruises and puffiness were finally going away, and he didn't much want to think about how they could sabotage Frankie. He probably should have. The way things turned out, maybe it would have been best for everybody if he had. But he didn't. There it was. He just didn't. It was like Samuel Kincaid's fist coming his way and him doing nothing to avoid it. The nudging pain in his belly for Frankie was continuing to grow, coming his way like a freight train gathering speed. But he was struck dumb in the headlights like a rabbit on the tracks, hypnotized by the light.

"Well, don't we?" Beth said again.

"Maybe we ought to just live and let live."

"But she's such a liar. All those stories about her fancy parents and her rich aunt. And she can't even read."

It was jealousy talking. Frankie had opened Ma up again. The family hadn't been able to do that for her after Tom's death, but Frankie had. Luke didn't much understand why Ma had taken to Frankie so quick like she did, but there it was. There had to be a reason. Ma probably knew something they didn't, he figured. Maybe Frankie shared some secret with her, or maybe Ma just needed some hurt little animal to love, to wipe away the numb feeling she'd had since Tom's death. Luke wished *he* had something to fill that hollow feeling he sometimes got late in the night thinking about Tom.

"Maybe we should just be happy Ma's better now," he finally said. "Maybe that's what we should be thinking about."

Luke ladled the last of the cream, tapped the tin top back onto the milk can, and carried the cream trough to the separate cooling room at the west end of the barn. It was a boxy little room that smelled like old socks, where balls of cheese wrapped in cloth hung from the ceiling to ripen. Ma would take care of the operation from here tomorrow. He laid a cloth over the wooden trough so no flies would get in it.

End of chores. Luke and Beth left the barn and walked back to the house. Twin wisps of smoke trailed out of chimneys at opposite ends.

Beth made one last try before they went in. "Don't you see how she's spoiling everything?"

They stopped at the foot of the porch, Luke shaking his head.

"Just leave it alone, Beth. It'll be okay."

She looked at him like she would Miss Nielson when she gave too much homework.

"You like her, don't you? That's why you got beat up for her. She's got you fooled, too. Well, she doesn't fool me."

She stomped up the steps and went inside. Luke stayed out on the porch for a bit. Beth was wrong. Frankie wasn't fooling him. He saw through her, but he wasn't quite sure what was on the other side. She was a mystery, like those dark corners in the barn at twilight. Every once in a while there would be a little scurrying motion, but you couldn't see in there—only guess at what was going on.

Frankie sat next to Ma at dinner, wearing a new navy blue pinafore. For the past few days Ma had actually sat down to meals with the family, instead of bustling around the kitchen to ignore the empty space at Tom's place.

"I don't know about this strike," Ma said as she passed the mashed potatoes to Beth. "Seems like those miners have got more money now than ever and plenty of free time to spend it in. A body could hardly walk down the streets of Trinidad today, they were that thick in town. And I have to tell you, Pa"—she sighed and plopped some butter onto her potatoes—"it smelled like a brewery all over town."

Pa glanced at Luke, rolling his eyes, then spooned out a big helping of overcooked canned green beans, the color of dried sagebrush.

"I don't know, Anne. I doubt if all those strikers have money to burn. The union's only giving them three dollars a week."

"And it's three dollars into the till at the Belle of Colorado saloon, I'm telling you."

Ma didn't think too highly of Pa giving away milk to the strikers. She didn't miss a chance to bad-mouth them. You'd think she'd never lost a son in the mines, the way she sided with the money people.

Beth was sitting sullen, hunched over her plate, with a face that looked like she smelled something pretty bad.

"Now sit up straight, Beth," Ma suddenly said. "Look how nice Francine sits."

Beth shot Frankie a look that would have given the devil collywobbles, but Frankie ignored her.

"You look real nice tonight, Francine," Pa said.

She did, too. Her hair was starting to grow out, and she combed it to the side. Short hair looked good on her, Luke thought. Natural.

"I thought the child needed some clothes," Ma said, looking at the new pinafore admiringly, and then went red in the face that she was making a fuss over the child.

"How come I didn't get a new one?" Beth said. "I had to wear last year's Easter dress the first day of school."

Ma looked flustered for a moment. "I know, honey."

Luke saw Ma's expression change. The old Tom sadness

came across her face, setting a cast to her eyes, turning her mouth down. It was like she suddenly realized it might not be so good to play favorites like she was, but again Luke couldn't help thinking Ma had a reason. She was being pulled between Beth and Francine, looking from one to the other quickly.

Then she set her jaw, like she made her mind up. "But you shouldn't begrudge others something nice, Beth. Francine here didn't have a stitch of clothing of her own."

"Well how come she didn't? How come she had to go around wearing boy's clothes?"

Pa spooned a double portion of the overdone beans onto Beth's plate like a kind of punishment. "You just eat up, young lady," he said, "and quit worrying about what doesn't concern you."

"It's not fair!"

This time she really meant it. Beth got up from the table, overturning her chair as she did so. She was in for it then. No one got up before Ma said it was okay. But Beth didn't wait for a scolding. She ran right upstairs and slammed her bedroom door behind her.

Ma sat in silence for a little, then shook her head. "I don't know what's getting into that girl. I blame it on lack of discipline at school." She turned to Luke. "That teacher of yours is too young."

She brought it all back around on Luke, like he was the one who'd hired Miss Nielson. But he didn't say anything. Suddenly he was beginning to agree with Beth: Maybe it wasn't fair. He hadn't had a new pair of shoes in a year, and the ones he had on now were not only wearing out but were so small for him that they were beginning to pinch the big toe of his left foot.

Ma looked at Frankie with a consoling smile on her face.

"Don't you pay any attention to her, Francine."

"I don't want to cause problems," Frankie said in her sweet-little-rich-girl voice. "Maybe I should go."

"Oh, no," Ma said quickly.

Luke almost said it with her. It was a sign of how much he was being sucked in by Frankie, worn-out shoes or not.

6

Next Saturday, Mother Jones came to Trinidad to talk. She was a legend in her own time: into her eighties, but still riding the rails all over the country, fighting for workingmen and -women and telling the bosses where to get off.

Pa, who had been pretty silent about the strike since the young Greek kid had been shot in custody, made some excuse about having to deliver milk early so as he and Luke could get into town to hear her. It was a man's outing, and Luke was happy for that. It was good to be away from the women for a time, especially Frankie. He just couldn't be himself when she was around. He was always trying to impress her or to figure her out. She got in your mind like cigarette smoke does in your clothes.

He was just thinking how good it was to be alone with Pa when suddenly there was a tapping at the back window, which made them both jump in their seats. It was Frankie, of course. Pa pulled over and she scrambled in front with them, taking the middle seat without complaint.

"Ma's going to give you a licking for this," Pa told her.

She just shook her head. "Don't think so."

Pa quick gave Luke a look that said What've we got here?

"You think you got her figured out?" Pa said, putting the truck in gear again.

"Maybe." She was wearing a red-and-black-plaid mackinaw and an old pair of Luke's overalls underneath. They still had some life because he'd grown out of them before wearing them out.

Luke sat up straight in the seat for the rest of the ride and set his jaw like he'd seen men do when they were being silent and strong. He figured most women liked that type of guy. It gave him a pain in the jaw muscle, though. That was Frankie's effect on him. He was always thinking how he looked to her, what she would think about him. So he played the strong, silent type, and by the time they got to town, his jaw muscle almost had a charley horse.

Trinidad was like a city to him. There must've been ten thousand people living there, and in some pretty fine buildings. There were big old brick-and-stone ones that housed hotels like the Toltec and the Columbian, others with fancy scrollwork decoration around the windows where the town's three newspapers and two theaters could be found. And there were also shops of all sorts with display windows nearly as big as the front of the barn back at the ranch. Most amazing of all to Luke, there were tall, electric lights over the paved streets and even wooden sidewalks so as you didn't have to share the street with the cars and carriages. There was just about everything in Trinidad, from the Mount San Rafael church and hospital at one end to Beckman's Brewery at the other.

Pa parked off Main, and the people were already congregating for Mother Jones's speech later that morning. There were hundreds of people all over the streets, most sporting the red bandanna that signified a striker. They even brought their wives and kids to hear Mother Jones. It was like a big picnic because the men knew she would put on a good show.

Sheriff Farr and his men were out, too, all along the

wooden sidewalks. And the Baldwin–Felts private detectives in their black suits and pointed boots, with bulges under the coats where they packed their guns—they were pretty thick on the ground, as well.

But there was no sign of trouble with the strikers. They'd just come for a good time, come to hear Mother Jones give the mine owners a tongue-lashing. They'd set up a grandstand for her right across from the downtown office of the CFI, with red, white, and blue banners hanging from poles like around a carnival booth. Pa, Luke, and Frankie got up right near the bandstand so they could get a good look at the little lady.

Pretty soon a crowd of men and women and some other kids filled in around them. The turnout was a heck of a lot higher than for the local baseball team, the Trinidad Trappers, and a whole lot more festive.

Then the people at the back of the crowd began to cheer and clap, and there was a sort of shuffling and pushing. As Luke looked over his shoulder to see what was going on, he noticed that Frankie had worked to the edge of the crowd, near where one of the private detectives was standing with his arms crossed over his barrel chest and a smirk on his face.

Luke didn't pay any more attention to her because now the reason for the cheering and the pushing was coming into sight. He could see two feathers on her hat before he caught a glimpse of her, but the ripples of people moving out of the way broke over them and shoved them aside to make way for Mother Jones, strutting smack down the middle of the crowd to reach the stand.

She looked like a grandmother, with white hair and little wire-rim glasses and wearing a neat-as-a-pin wool suit. And there on her right, wearing a checkered cap, a coat and tie, and leather leggings, was Louis Tikas, sent down from

Denver by the union to organize things at Ludlow. Luke had met him last week on a milk run, and he seemed a nice enough guy. Ma, of course, called him a jumped-up Greek because he owned a coffeehouse. Well, these two brushed right by Pa and Luke, and Tikas winked at Luke as they passed. Then he said a few words to Mother Jones as she was climbing up the rough wooden steps to the platform, and she turned and nodded at Pa. Luke glanced at Pa, who was going all red in the face. First time he ever saw him like that.

Up on the platform, Mother Jones tucked right into her speech like a hungry miner to a steak dinner. No pussy-footing around and joking for her.

"Are you men or cowards?" she called out from the front rail of the stand.

"Men!" came the cry back from the crowd.

"Then we'll win this strike. A woman likes a good man. This woman likes a good man."

They cheered that one, too, and one of the guys in the crowd yelled up, "How about a date?" It was in good humor and she laughed a little, but then she got very serious, pulling her hat down tighter over her forehead. She told the crowd how they were going to win the strike by keeping the mines shut.

"There aren't enough scabs to fill your jobs. But when they come . . ."

"They're already here," shouted another guy from the back of the crowd.

"Well, God bless," she said. "The early bird catches the worm."

Even Pa laughed at this. There was a bit of backslapping and nodding of heads; then Mother Jones went back on the attack.

"So they're here and you've got to educate them. Let

them know what the operators are up to. Strike-breaking. That's what. How many of you boys came as scabs the last strike?"

Luke looked around at the question, and a lot of men suddenly had their eyes fixed on a point about two inches in front of their boots.

"No need to answer that one," Mother Jones went on. "But look at us now. United. Brothers and sisters in the fight. That's what we've got to do with the men the operators bring in. Educate them. Treat them like brothers."

There were a whole lot more good things, too. But Luke got distracted watching Frankie working around the edges of the crowd and going behind some man, getting lost from sight, then sort of wandering back to the edges again, like she was checking cattle at the fair.

Luke lost track of her for a time and suddenly there came a rousing, shrill cry from the bandstand as Mother Jones wrapped her speech up:

"And, boys, remember this as the months pass by. You've got to pray for the dead, but fight like hell for the living!"

You'd have thought the Trinidad Trappers just won their first home game in a decade the way the people carried on. They were cheering, clapping, and shouting all at once. Hats were flying in the air and men were hugging each other. It was the strangest thing Luke ever saw. Watching out for Frankie, he must have missed something. It was a good talk, all right, but he didn't feel like hugging anybody over it. Pa decided to rumple his hair. That was about the extent of his show of emotion. Luke looked up at his pa and saw he was grinning wide enough to show the brown stains on his front teeth from drinking artesian well water.

"You've just witnessed greatness, Luke," Pa said. "I hope you always remember this day."

At that moment, he seemed as happy as Luke had ever seen him, but his eyes squinted as he looked around quickly.

"Where's that girl?"

Luke pointed in the direction of a Baldwin–Felts man. "She was roaming around the crowd last I saw her."

"Well, let's find her before everybody starts leaving. She could get trampled."

Luke didn't have any fears along those lines. Frankie, he figured, was the foot, not the ground, the type to be walking over you, not vice versa.

Pa and he went in different directions, agreeing to meet up at Kincaid's Dry Goods. It didn't take Luke long to find her. She was hanging around a group of men in jackets and ties, and she had that same look of livestock appraiser on her face as before. She caught sight of Luke and quick changed her expression and ran over to him.

"I got lost," she said.

He was about to say sure you did, but she took his hand in hers.

"Just till we get out of the crowd, okay?"

He nodded, speechless. A lump the size of a plum blocked his throat. A blizzard of butterflies was playing in his stomach. He took the long route out of the crowd, holding on to her hand as long as he could. It felt so soft and warm. There weren't any callouses on her palm or fingers. Tender as a cow's udder.

7

Pa was waiting for them at Kincaid's, scratching his head and craning his neck, but he'd been joined by Ben Green from the neighboring farm. Pa gave Frankie a little bit of a scolding—he couldn't be strict with her any more than Ma could—and Luke said he'd keep an eye on her while Pa talked with Mr. Green.

Pa never had liquor around the house, but Luke knew he liked to maybe visit a saloon when in town and talk with old friends. So Frankie and Luke wandered around town for a while. The plan was to meet back at the truck at two.

Frankie wanted to go into Kincaid's, and he followed along, none too eager to give Samuel's dad any of his business. The place was packed with ladies doing Saturday shopping. Luke looked around to see if Samuel was helping his dad out today, and when he turned back, Frankie was gone again. She was like a rabbit or something. You couldn't take your eyes off her for an instant. He tried to move past the women, but they only glared at him. Short of getting on his hands and knees and crawling under their skirts down the aisles, there was nothing he could do to track her down. He was pretty sure Frankie hadn't gone back out of the store, so he just waited at the entrance for her to leave.

It took a good fifteen minutes.

"You get lost again?" Luke said as she approached.

She shrugged. "Just looking."

Back out on the street they were taking the bandstand down. There were still plenty of men around, talking in lots of different languages.

"Want a licorice?"

Luke looked at her outstretched hand. She was offering a couple of licorice drops.

"I don't want to take your last ones," he said.

"You won't. I've got more in here." She opened the pocket flap on the mackinaw, and he looked inside. It was like the contents of a tiny candy counter in there.

"Where the heck did you get all those?"

She looked at him as if he'd been kicked in the head by a horse at birth.

"Where do you expect? Kincaid's."

"That must have cost a buck at least."

"No. Free. Saturday special."

It took a moment to sink in. "You mean you stole them?"

"Shh." She looked around to make sure no one had overheard. The men around were too busy talking to give them any notice.

She thrust her hand at him, holding the licorice drops under his nose.

"Just think of Samuel Kincaid when you eat these. Sweet revenge."

Luke was shocked at first. Stealing was something right up there with lying to your parents. But she kept holding the licorice under his nose and grinning at him until he finally found himself grinning back. There *was* a sort of sweet revenge to it, he thought, as he tossed the licorice in his mouth and sucked. It wasn't exactly his way to fight a battle, but what the heck. Sucking soon turned to chewing, with little bits of licorice lodging between his teeth. He knew he'd be tasting that bitter sweetness all afternoon.

They wandered around town some more, but he now kept a real close eye on Frankie if they went into a store.

Along about one-thirty they noticed a crowd of men gathering at the train station, so they walked over to see what was going on. Louis Tikas was in the crowd, and Luke went up to him.

"What's going on, Mr. Tikas?"

"You go on, now, son," he said. "This is no place for you."

Frankie peeked her head around a man's arm.

"No place for the girl, either. Go home."

"But what's happening?" Luke asked, more curious now because of his concern.

"A train is coming, that is what is happening. And on that train are eighteen gunfighters from New Mexico, hired by the mine owners. They send killers to us."

Luke's eyes got bigger. "Gunslingers coming here?"

"So you kids get on away."

"But what are you going to do?" Luke looked at the other men closely. Hardly any of them were carrying weapons.

Tikas smiled broadly at the question. "Just like Mother Jones says. We treat them like brothers. We educate them."

This Luke had to see.

"Now go on home," Tikas said, shooing them with his hands like you would an animal.

Luke took Frankie's hand and pulled her away from the crowd.

"But I want to see," she kept saying.

He kept a tight hold on her until they got around the far corner of the station, out of sight of Tikas.

"Let me go!"

He dropped her hand. "Look, I want to see it, too, but we do it this way. I don't want Mr. Tikas talking to Pa."

She stopped pouting. "You really care about what your pa says or does?"

"What kind of question is that? He's my pa."

"He's just a man. What makes him your boss?"

He'd never thought of it like that before. These were not questions you asked.

"He's my pa" was all he could come up with.

Frankie favored him once again with her pitying look.

The train pulled in then, snorting and puffing like a bull, disgorging its passengers. But you couldn't see this. The tracks were hidden by the station. The men waited patiently outside, waited even as the train pulled out of town. Finally, from the main doors of the station came a whole flock of men dressed in long oilskin duster coats with cowboy hats on that looked real fresh, no sweat stains or busted brims. These were fancy cowboys, Luke knew. Their boots were low, meant for walking and not riding.

They stopped all jammed up together by the station door, staring at the crowd of men waiting for them.

"Hello, brothers," Louis Tikas said.

The gunslingers just looked at one another with tight grins on their faces, then back at the crowd in front of them. There must have been a couple hundred men there. You could almost hear the calculations going through the minds of those gunslingers: six bullets per gun times eighteen guns.

"We have come to talk with you," Tikas went on.

A big black roadster pulled up now, and a couple of mine officials, along with Sheriff Farr and three guards, got out, but the crowd blocked them off from the gunslingers.

"Maybe you come with us to our hall? We talk. We have

food." Tikas was still smiling, but the gunslingers had stopped grinning.

The crowd slowly encircled those eighteen men, and the mine officials and Sheriff Farr were running helplessly around the fringes like dogs yapping at lost sheep.

Luke kept waiting for shots, but nothing happened. The gunslingers were completely swallowed up by the mass of men. Soon this circle of humanity started moving in unison back onto Main Street and on to the Union Hall, taking the gunslingers with them. It was a pretty slick maneuver.

Frankie and Luke followed along the side of the street, keeping up with the men but also keeping their distance. Luke had a funny feeling in the pit of his stomach that something big was going to happen. Those gunslingers weren't going to be pushed around. Or were they?

At the Union Hall, Frankie and he managed to sneak in with the crowd. It was a big old auditorium where union officials held speeches and even dances. A piano sat just next to the stage. Usually there were wooden seats arranged in rows, but now they were all folded and resting against a wall near the piano.

Slowly the mass of men dissolved and the eighteen gunslingers came into view again, their faces pinched and eyes narrowed like they were about ready to go down fighting.

"Brothers," Tikas said from the stage. "There is nothing to be afraid of."

"This is kidnapping," one of the gunmen said. He'd folded his duster back over his hip so that his gun was exposed. A wiry little guy, he stood with his entire body tensed while his right hand twitched over the butt of his holstered pistol.

Some of the other gunslingers said the same. Another one, who looked like some kind of cartoon of the Grim Reaper, with a long, hawk nose and skin the color of dead flesh, made a simple declaration:

"You've got two minutes, 'brother.' Then we walk."

The strikers didn't like this any, and one guy said low, "Heck with educating. Let's just kill 'em."

Luke looked for Frankie, but once again she was gone. A sudden panic came over him. This was all going wrong. Dead wrong. He could feel the tension mounting. Tikas was right: They shouldn't be here. Now Frankie was nowhere to be seen, and if anything started and she got hurt . . . He didn't even want to think of that one.

But he didn't want to make any fast moves, either, afraid the gunslingers would misunderstand. Tikas stood on the stage, trying to explain what the situation was—that the mine owners had brought them in to help break a strike—but he couldn't be heard very well for the murmurs and threats coming from both sides now. Luke started looking for a likely hiding place in case of a gunfight, when suddenly somebody started playing the piano by the stage. It was something slow and dirgelike, something you'd hear at church. Nobody paid much attention to it at first, the playing was so timid. Luke angled around men to get more to the side of things and drew closer to the piano as well.

The Grim-Reaper gunslinger shouted up at Tikas that this wasn't no church meeting. They didn't need no hymn music.

It seemed like Tikas only then heard the piano. Luke followed his gaze down to the piano and saw that it was Frankie there playing. Tikas waved at her to stop, but she kept her eyes on the keys as she began to play louder and more confidently.

"Time's ticking away, 'brother,' " the Grim Reaper said. The other gunslingers folded their long coats back, exposing their holstered weapons.

Frankie stopped playing, and for a moment the hall was deadly silent. There was a metallic, bitter smell in the air like before an electrical storm.

"We don't want violence," Tikas said. "We only want to explain."

"You got yourself about twenty seconds' worth of explaining time left," the little wiry gunslinger said.

Now Frankie started playing the piano again, but this time it was incredible, syncopated, happy music filling the place. Piano, but piano like Luke had never heard played before, all cheery and light and full of joy. The gunslingers squinted their eyes at it, their hands tensed over their guns. But as the music got livelier and louder, the Grim Reaper's hand sort of relaxed. He squinted at the men circling him, and he looked up at Tikas and finally over to the piano where Frankie was pounding out the lively rhythm. A little lizard grin turned his lips up at the corners for a second.

The other gunslingers and the strikers suddenly got that what-the-heck look on their faces. As they all turned to the piano, Frankie smiled back at them over her shoulder like it was the most natural thing in the world for her to be there, her little hands just flying over the keys.

"I'll be darned," the Grim Reaper finally said.

The men just stood there quiet for a time, until one striker started clapping his hands in time to the music and sort of square danced with another guy. Frankie kept on playing, making that old piano hop to the notes. She finished off this first number, and then one of the gunslingers called out a tune and sure enough, she could play that one, too. Suddenly the electric tension in the hall had broken, replaced by a wary joy.

"By God, she's a good one," a red-faced striker near Luke said.

"It's ragtime," his buddy said. "I haven't heard playing like that since my last visit to Madam Floe's in Denver." They both laughed with that kind of smugness men have when sharing a secret.

Luke didn't know what Madam Floe's was, but Frankie

sure sounded professional. He felt all the tension leaving him, too, and his right foot began tapping out time to the strange pulsing rhythm. He could see a couple of the gunslingers tapping their feet to the music now, too, pointing and laughing at the young girl pounding away on the ivories for all she was worth. Then Tikas jumped off the stage and walked right up to the Grim Reaper and thrust out his trim hand. The Grim Reaper looked warily at it for a minute.

"Don't worry," Tikas said. "I washed it this morning."

The Grim Reaper's lips curled up even higher in a smile with this, and the two shook hands. Cautious-like, but it was a shake.

After that, the strikers just gathered around and talked with the gunslingers as if they really were brothers, and the gunslingers listened. Finally, they voted among themselves then and there to take the next train out of town.

"We're not going to be hired guns for coal barons like the Rockefellers," the Grim Reaper said as they left.

The cheering and hurrahs were as loud for them as they had been for Mother Jones. And there was a good long round of it for Frankie, as well, led by Louis Tikas.

"Where the heck you learn to play like that?" Luke asked Frankie later as they were leaving the Union Hall.

She didn't look at him. "Places."

"Boy, you were great."

"It's easy," she said, but there was a kind of trembling in her voice that he could not understand. She was a hero. How come she was so sad?

Luke told Pa all about their adventure when they met up back at the truck. Had to, because he figured Pa would hear of it from someone else if he didn't. Pa wasn't any too pleased at first, but he finally gave both of them a big hug, squeezing them to his chest.

"Like Mother Jones says." He grinned, holding them

back out at arm's length. "Pray for the dead and fight like hell for the living."

Ma was less understanding, of course. Both Frankie and Luke went to bed without supper. Up in his room, Luke could still see the smile on Beth's face as Ma laid into them for being disobedient. Beth was pretty happy, all right, because Frankie was finally getting her comeuppance.

It was late that night when a tap came at his door once again. This time Luke didn't waste a second getting to it, but still the hall was empty. On the floor in front of his door lay a little pile of candy: some powdery mints, licorice drops, and root beer suckers. He quickly scooped them up and underneath found a little black leather wallet. Flipping it open, he discovered a metal star inside: a deputy sheriff's badge. Luke gathered the candy and wallet in his hands and went back into the room. He lay on the bed half the night, rationing the sweets and trying to figure out Frankie. Now he knew what she'd been doing wandering around in the crowd this morning. She wasn't lost, just looking for victims with loose pockets.

The more Luke thought about all of it—her phony story about coming from a wealthy New York family, her lack of schooling but incredible talent with the piano and thieving—the more he knew he had to get to the bottom of her mystery.

8

By the middle of October the undeclared war between strikers and the mine guards and Baldwin–Felts men had broken out into a real shootout. The private detectives drove their armored car into another, smaller tent colony up at Forbes one day, and the jittery guard manning the car's gun panicked when he saw some miners coming at him with rifles in their hands. They were just returning from hunting jackrabbits, but the guard didn't know this and opened fire. He killed a couple of miners and badly injured a kid not much older than Luke.

That was all the men needed. They took to the hills, attacking any CFI transport they could and even shooting up a guards' barracks.

The result was that good men on both sides died and there were no more trips to Ludlow for Luke, Frankie, and Beth before school. Pa still made the milk run in the mornings, but early, before the family ate breakfast. Luke was itching to see what was going on at the camp, but Ma wouldn't hear of any of them getting within a mile of the place.

It was like living in a war zone. Pa made the kids crouch down on the floorboards of the cab as they drove back and forth between school and home. Stray bullets didn't know whose side you were on, he said.

Luke, Beth, and Frankie would hear rumors at school, or Pa would tell them news about the strike; otherwise, they were cut off completely from what was going on. The kitchen clock ticked noisily at night while Luke tried to concentrate on his homework; the overhead kerosene lamp hissed; and all he could think about was those men, women, and children out in the tents with only canvas to protect them.

Meanwhile, the battle between Beth and Frankie continued at home, despite the fact that Pa even attempted to intervene.

"You don't much like Francine, do you?" he said to Beth as they were finishing the milking one day out in the barn.

She didn't answer, just set her little jaw and stuck out her lips in a pout.

"Well, what are we going to do about it?" he said. "Can't keep up with this sniping and bickering all the time."

Luke was about to suggest that maybe they all sit down and hash it out over dinner when Beth blurted:

"I say send her back where she came from."

Pa blinked once and shook his head. It was going to be harder than he thought.

"Can't really do that now, can we?"

"Why not?" Beth said.

"Don't know where she came from."

"New York," Beth said. "Least that's what she says."

Pa sighed. "And what if we couldn't send her back? What if it wouldn't be a good thing to do? For Francine?"

Pa was trying to get at something, but Luke was darned if he could figure out what.

"Maybe if we did some stuff together," Luke said, "we'd all feel more like friends."

Pa smiled at this. "That's what I was thinking, son. Together." Then he looked at Beth. She was not convinced. "You know it doesn't mean we love you any less, sweetie. But you got to help people sometimes. It's part of what makes us human."

Beth was about to cave in, Luke could see—her eyes were filming over and her lips were starting to quiver—when Pa added:

"And she's made your ma come to life again. That's a blessing."

Beth wiped her eyes at this and set her stubborn jaw again. The chance had been missed.

"You'll help out, won't you, sweetie?"

"Sure, Pa," Beth said. But the flat way she said it told Luke no truce had been won.

It was a couple weeks later and another one of those soft pink twilights that come in late fall. Beth and Luke were in the barn doing the skimming again, and the cats were swarming around their legs, curling and rubbing and meowing. Luke was trying to keep his mind on the job and not pay any attention to Beth's loud silence. She'd been brooding for the past several days, going around with this black bag of meanness on her back like some evil Santa Claus. And they'd all been avoiding her because of it. Frankie was fitting in, becoming part of the family. So nobody wanted to hear Beth's gripes anymore, least of all Luke.

They just worked together quiet-like, Beth steadying the heavy wooden trough as he took his turn at ladling the globs of cream out of the milk urn. The cats were so insistent that Luke couldn't even move to get a better angle on the milk for skimming. Tension had obviously been building in him, though, without him even knowing it, because suddenly he kicked one of the cats to get it out from underfoot. It squealed and tumbled into a dark corner with the force of the kick.

"Out of the way, Pokey."

"It's Petunia," Beth said. "And you shouldn't be kicking her. She didn't do anything to you."

Luke was about to make the same comparison to Frankie when into the barn she walked.

Frankie didn't say anything at first, just sort of poked around the stalls and fingered the hoes and rakes hanging on the plank walls between wooden pegs.

"Hey," Luke said, stopping the ladling for a moment.

But Beth only bristled at Frankie's presence. "We got to get the cream out, Luke, before it goes bad."

Frankie looked their way, as if only then noticing them.

"Want some help?" she asked.

It was like a truce flag being offered. Luke waited a second for Beth to get the picture and accept, but she just stuck out her lips and squinted her eyes.

"Sure," Luke said for both of them. "That'd be great."

"It's a two-person job," Beth said, without even looking up from the trough.

"Come on, Beth," he said. "She's just trying to pitch in."

This comment was like some signal for Beth, like Luke was taking sides, and it set her off faster than a Fourth of July rocket.

"Well, let her pitch in somewhere she's wanted."

And with that, Beth picked up the nearly full wooden trough of cream and threw it at Frankie, who neatly jumped aside. The thing landed with a bang and a high, piercing squeal.

"Beth! You've hit one of the cats."

Luke ran over to where the cat lay, but there was

60

nothing to be done. Its head was all caved in. The other cat came over now and started licking cream lying on the ground. When Beth came close, Luke got up and held her back.

"You don't want to see it."

"Let me go." She wiggled free and bent over to pick up the body. One of its eyes was dangling out of the socket, and there was gray, sticky stuff oozing from the wound on its head.

Beth stood cradling it like a doll and began sobbing.

"Oh, Petunia," she said, tears streaming down her face. "Petunia, Petunia."

Frankie and Luke looked at each other, and there was a single moment of recognition, of seeing yourself in the other. They were brought together in that moment by shame and pity.

"It's all your fault," Beth spluttered.

"Beth." Luke could only stare at her. "She was trying to help out. You're the one threw the trough."

"Oh, sure." She spun on him. "Take her side. Just like Ma and Pa. Everybody's on her side."

"Beth," began Frankie. "I really . . ."

But Beth wouldn't let her finish. "I wish you'd never come here. I wish it every night."

She turned and stomped out of the barn, the cat still in her arms.

They buried Petunia later that night out back near where Spunky, the old sheepdog, had been planted. Pa and Luke dug the hole deep so as no scavengers would dig it up. Pokey had come out of the barn and sat, almost invisible in the shadows cast by their lantern, watching every shovelful come out. Beth was in her room, still sobbing. They could hear her way out back.

*   *   *

61

Ma was the one finally to do something about the situation. She wrote to her sister, Polly, in Denver, and in a couple more days a reply came: Aunt Polly would love to have Beth visit for a time.

You knew things were desperate when Ma asked Polly for any help. Polly was the smart one in the family: a college graduate and a social worker up in Denver. She was married but didn't have any kids. Ma said she pushed her husband, Carl, around something awful, and maybe she did. She was real big, and he was tiny as a sparrow and worked as an accountant.

Aunt Polly was the kind of relative who sent books of famous sayings for your birthday or underwear for Christmas. Luke didn't think Beth deserved to be sent there. She'd been a pain, all right, and it would be a relief for all of the family for her to be gone for a spell, but he didn't feel too good about it.

"With these strikers shooting everything that moves, nobody's safe around here lately," Ma said by way of explanation at dinner the night she got the letter from Denver. "I don't want a child of mine in the line of fire. It'll be for just a little while, Beth. Until things calm down around here."

"Why aren't you sending Luke, too?" Beth asked. "He's your child."

"Luke's older, and we need him around here to help out. You'll have fun with your aunt."

"It really isn't fair, Ma," Luke finally said, but he did not say it with much conviction.

"It's not a punishment," Ma said to him. "You kids make it sound like Siberia." She smiled at Beth. "This is an opportunity for you, honey. The big city. Fancy stores. You'll like it. I've been meaning to send you there for a long time."

Beth scowled across the table at Frankie. Everybody knew what was going through her mind, but nobody, not even Beth, said it.

"Could be a new dress in it for you," Pa said, but there wasn't much enthusiasm in his voice, either.

They all sat there like at a funeral. Frankie kept her eyes on her plate, saying not a word. Luke couldn't figure it out. He didn't know why Ma and Pa were taking Frankie's side against Beth. It was like there was some big thing that nobody wanted to say, so they all sat there until the half-eaten food got cold and then drifted away from the table.

Later that night, when Luke gave his ma a hug before going up to bed, she whispered in his ear, "You'll understand later, Luke. Things are hard, but it's for the best."

Late afternoon of the next day they took her to the train. Just Luke and Ma, who would accompany Beth to Denver. Frankie stayed at the ranch. Pa couldn't stand good-byes no more than he could thank you's. He just dropped them off at the Ludlow station real quick.

"Got business to tend to," he said, not even looking at Beth. "See you soon, punkin."

And he was gone before Beth could pull her hand out of her mitten to wave good-bye. Luke put an arm around her shoulder, and she actually allowed it for a time. Ma was busy getting the tickets in order. They looked north toward the tent colony. This was the first time they'd been near it in a couple of weeks. Across the tracks from the strikers' tents now was a little encampment of khaki-colored conical ones—the state militia. Governor Ammons had called them in finally at the end of October, and so far the peace had been kept without the militia taking the side of the mine owners or the strikers.

Instead, they were starting to take the guns away from both sides. Luke didn't know if Beth had heard this or not, but it made Ma's excuse for sending her away even dumber.

"She's spoiling everything, Luke," Beth suddenly said. "Don't you know that?"

He patted her shoulder, acting like he hadn't heard.

"You're going to have a great time in Denver. Wish I could go."

She finally shrugged his arm off her shoulder and looked him cold in the eye.

"You know what I mean. She tries to worm her way in everywhere. To fool everybody. But she doesn't fool me."

"Beth . . ." he began.

"She doesn't fool me, Luke. Hear?" Her voice grew to an outraged shout.

Ma looked around at them from the ticket counter where she was gabbing with Miss Hollearan, daughter of the owners of the land where the strikers were camping.

Beth gazed downward at her dress-up shoes. She had all her best clothes on: the Sunday coat and navy blue dress and even a little hat with a feather, which made her look like a midget grown-up.

"She doesn't fool me," she hissed.

Luke let it be for a time until from the distance he heard the hoot of the train from Trinidad.

"We should just make peace," he finally said. "Try to put the past behind us."

But she shook her head, making the little curls Ma had so painstakingly put in her hair flop about her face.

"That's what she tried." Beth fixed him with her cold stare again. "Putting those stupid gifts outside my door. A biscuit or some candies. Even a deputy sheriff's badge.

Well, how did she get all those things, that's what I want to know."

It felt like a cold hand was reaching into Luke's chest.

"She was trying to buy me off with those," Beth said. "To be my friend." She smiled at him suddenly, like a fellow conspirator. "But I just passed them along to you. Serves her right."

She gave a nasty little giggle at this, and Luke tasted a sourness in the back of his throat, a burning bitterness like he was about to puke.

"That was you?" he said.

She nodded. "Course it was. Who'd you think?"

Ma bustled over to them, waving the tickets.

"Train's coming. You got all your bags?"

There were three of them, gathered around their legs in a semicircle. Ma carried the lunch basket with egg salad sandwiches and a corked bottle full of warm tea. The train was pulling into the station now, and Ma hugged Luke tight.

"I'll be back in a couple of days. You take care of your pa. Hear?"

He nodded dumbly, still trying to get a hold on what Beth had told him.

"Give your sister a hug, boy," Ma said.

Luke leaned over and sort of gripped Beth's shoulders, but he didn't look into her face.

"She never even knew I gave her gifts away," Beth whispered.

Then they got on the train, found some seats in the second-class compartment, and waved as the train pulled out.

The Denver express was way down the line past the arroyo when Luke finally realized that he was holding a limp hand upright in a miserable attempt at a wave.

He felt in his pocket for the little black wallet containing the badge, checked around the platform to make sure nobody was looking, then pulled the wallet out and dropped it in the trash bucket by the exit.

Pa would be back to pick him up in a few minutes.

9

By the time they got back to the ranch that evening, Luke was feeling pretty confused. He figured it really didn't matter who'd given him those little presents outside his door. What did matter was that he'd automatically thought they came from Frankie and not from his own sister. He'd been making things up about Frankie, making her out to be better than she was. Apart from those gifts, which weren't even from her, what was there to show that she really gave half a thought to him? he wondered. A look now and again, him reading her expression to mean something maybe it didn't mean at all. Her taking his hand that day in Trinidad—but that could've been just to distract him so he didn't catch her thieving.

Pa pulled up in front of the house. Lights were on inside. "We'd better get the dinner," he said, slipping out of the truck. But Luke stayed in there for a minute, figuring.

He'd thought Frankie liked him, that she was trying to say thanks in her own way with the candy and badge. Now he didn't know. Maybe Beth was right; maybe Frankie was trying to worm her way in, to ruin things in the family. She'd sure been successful with Beth. She had come between Luke and his own sister, had separated Beth out of the family herd like a good sheepdog at work. And now Beth was up in Denver. Would he be next?

"You coming, Luke?" Pa called from the top of the front steps.

Luke got out of the truck and headed toward the house.

It's a funny thing about suspicion: Once you open up to it, the whole world matches those suspicions. Everything seems to fit the evil outline you lay down. It's like the world is a big mirror for your bad thoughts.

Opening the front door, they were greeted by a hearty, spicy aroma coming from the kitchen, a sort of mix of pot roast and pumpkin pie. Smelling it, Luke suddenly realized just how hungry he was. In the excitement of getting Beth off to Denver, none of them had eaten a proper meal all day.

Pa squinted at Luke, a half grin on his lips. "Ma must've left something to heat up."

In the kitchen they found Frankie at the stove, wearing Ma's apron and tending a bubbling pot. The good smell was coming from the oven. They both stood there for a moment, watching Frankie without her knowing they were home, watching as she stirred the contents of the pot. She did it with such a delicate touch that it hardly looked like cooking at all as compared to the way Ma bustled around the kitchen banging pots and pans. Where Ma attacked the food, Frankie petted it. Luke felt the nudging tug in his guts just watching her but resolved this time not to be won over.

Instead, he said he'd got a bellyache and went on up to bed early.

It was impossible for him to sleep that night. He had a feeling in his stomach like he did the night before a big test at school, a test he hadn't studied for. He'd close his eyes, and there would be Beth with the dead cat in her arms, looking at him with eyes all red from crying. Then he'd roll over on his other side, squinching his eyes tight and crushing a pillow over his head, and there was Frankie with

Ma's apron on, sitting in Ma's rocker and staring into the dying embers of the fire so that the orange glow didn't just reflect in her eyes; it looked like it was coming from them. Onto his back then and breathing deep with the pillow off his head, and there was Pa with the strikers, talking to them in their language, wearing a red bandanna around his neck.

"The heck with it," he finally said out loud and sat up in bed, propping the pillows behind him. He could hear Pa snoring down the hall, hear the wind picking up outside, whistling over the tableland, rattling the screens on the downstairs windows. He reached over, lit his kerosene lamp, and turned the wick down low. Then he leaned back to watch the light from the tiny flame pulsing on the ceiling.

There was a creaking sound from the hallway, and he listened more closely. Pa was still snoring, but there came the creak again from loose floorboards. A gentle rap at his door.

"Luke, you awake?"

His head jerked toward the door, but he didn't answer. She didn't knock again, but she opened the door softly, peeking her head in. Their eyes met and she nodded at him, then came into the room, shutting the door behind her. She was barefoot and dressed in a floor-length flannel nightgown that buttoned up the front. He tried to take his eyes from her feet but couldn't as she moved toward his bed. They were long and skinny feet, and seeing them was like erasing some of her magic, like feeling disappointment and relief all at once. Just flesh and bone, he thought. Just like me. She wore a plaster on her right little toe.

"Why didn't you answer?" She stopped a couple feet from his bed.

"I don't know."

She folded her arms across her chest at this. "I thought we were friends."

He shrugged, beginning to feel awful stupid sitting up in bed while she was standing there. But he didn't feel like getting out. He couldn't remember if his nightshirt was clean or not.

"What's the matter with you?" she said.

"It wasn't right they sent Beth away." But he didn't look directly at her.

She sighed, re-crossing her arms. "So that's it. I didn't notice you making any big protests about it. Seems to me everybody was relieved to get rid of her."

"That's not true."

She cocked her head at him. "No? Then you tell me what's true."

"It's like you're trying to take over. Get rid of Beth, get rid of Ma—"

"I give up." She dropped her arms in disgust. "I didn't get rid of anybody, least of all your ma. She's coming back in two days."

"Wearing her apron, doing the cooking." He felt the heat in his cheeks and knew his face was turning bright red like it did when he got agitated.

She shook her head in disbelief. "This is crazy. I make you a dinner and you think I'm moving in. I thought you'd like it, that you'd want to have some nice smells around the place when your ma was gone. Make it like a home. Make it like a thank you for all your ma's done for me."

There was a ball of emotion growing in his throat, about to suffocate him unless it burst loose.

"So maybe I was wrong about Ma," he allowed. "But that doesn't make it okay about Beth. Doesn't make it all right for you to come here and sneak right in to be favorite, to turn Ma's head so that she sends her own daughter away."

It was partly his own guilt speaking, guilt that he hadn't made a protest to save Beth. Frankie was right: He had been relieved Beth was sent away. And the guilt spilled out not just in his words but in his tone, sharp and cutting as a barbershop razor.

Frankie staggered backward a step as if hit. She sniffed once and then looked hard at him, turning her head a bit to the side like a snake will before it strikes.

"So that's what you think? That I'm sneaking in."

"With all your stupid stories about your rich parents when it's as plain as noonday sun what you really are."

A flicker of jaw muscle. "And what's that?" she asked.

But he was lost now. That was as far as his thoughts had gone.

Outside, the wind was blowing harder. A door had come loose on the barn and was knocking back and forth against its jamb. Frankie started nodding her head like she'd made up her mind about something.

"Okay," she said. "You're the one who wants to know everything. To find out all the secrets." She put her hand to the top button of her nightdress and slowly unbuttoned it. "To figure out what makes everybody tick." Her hand went to the second button, and she undid it as well.

Luke tried to swallow, but it stuck in his throat. His fingernails dug into his palms as he continued to clench his fists.

"What do you think you're doing?"

She smiled then, that grin of hers from the lips only. "I'm going to satisfy your curiosity."

A third button. He could see the white skin just below her collarbone. It had a blue cast to it from veins close to the surface.

71

"Pa'll skin us both if he finds us," Luke said. His mouth was so dry his tongue stuck to the roof of it when he spoke.

She met his eyes and held them with hers, her hands still at work on the buttons. Then suddenly, in one movement, she spun around and pulled the nightdress down her back some. Luke stared, his eyes bulging, the ball of emotion in his throat cracking into a hoarse groan.

"What're those?" He reached over and turned the wick up. Now he could see the welts clearly, red and puckered, forming a crisscross pattern on her back like the footprints a crow leaves in the snow. "Who did that to you?"

Frankie pulled the flannel gown up over her shoulders once again and turned to him, her face blank like a mask, all except for her jaw muscles and the vein throbbing at her temple. She buttoned the nightgown primly up to her neck.

"Any more questions?"

"Ma saw those?" Luke asked.

She nodded.

"That's why she's being so protective about you."

"Could be. Having somebody care what happens to me is a new experience, and that's for sure."

Neither of them said anything for several moments. Pa's snoring was like the distant chuffing of a freight train.

Finally she turned and left without another word. Luke listened to her footsteps creaking down the hall. He blew out the light several minutes later, but the crisscross scarring lingered on his eyes like the final blink of light after the sun goes down.

10

They lay huddled behind a little hillock overlooking the water station on the Colorado and Southern line about a mile from the ranch. The Sunday run should be coming in about five minutes. Secretly, Luke hoped they'd missed it. But he wasn't going to chicken out. He felt there was a bond between him and Frankie after he had seen those scars.

"Now you just follow me," Frankie said in a whisper. "It's a lot of fun; you'll see." There wasn't a soul about for miles, but she had to whisper like they were some war party or something.

"How come it has to be the last car?"

She gave him that pitying look again. "So's if you don't make it, the other cars don't run over you."

The fear must have shown on his face then, for she quickly added, "Don't worry. Just follow me. It's a cinch."

Hawks played overhead, riding the air drafts, swooping up and down and calling out to one another. Luke couldn't ever remember them seeming playful before. It was a cold day for hopping a freight train, and they'd both bundled up in mackinaws and gloves. The ground was chill where they lay, coming through their clothes, digging right into their bones. A low gray sky overhead. He looked at the landscape as if for the first time: the black-scarred hillsides ahead of them dotted by dirty smudges of pinyon pines; the flat, brownish tableland and arroyos; and the rusty tracks cutting through it all. Frankie suddenly began working her hands together, beating her legs against the ground.

"Got to keep limber," she explained. "We'll only have a couple seconds when it comes down to it."

The low whistle sounded then, filling their lonely cutting with its song, sending goose bumps all over Luke's neck.

"Here she comes," he said, trying to break through his fear.

Frankie just shook her head at such an obvious statement. "You'd make a great scout."

It was a short train come up from Trinidad and before that God only knew where. Aside from one trip to Denver, Luke had never been out of the southern coalfields. Every other place seemed exotic to him, even New Mexico, which was close by. And suddenly, seeing the train coming around the curve toward them, steam pouring out its funnel, the rhythmic clacking of its wheels over the tracks blotting out all other sound, even the anxious pounding of his heart, Luke's fear began to disappear. It was replaced by a new emotion: excitement. More than any other tangible object in the universe, the train represented adventure to Luke. Freedom. And here it was, coming his way finally.

Frankie hugged the ground as the train pulled to a stop under the water tower. Luke could now see why they weren't directly by the water tower itself. She'd positioned them perfectly, toward the rear of the train, where they'd have to make their mad dash for the last car just as the train was leaving.

"Get down." She tugged his shoulder to the ground. He could smell the coal dust, watched a pill bug make its awkward way in front of his nose.

He sneaked a peek every now and again as he heard the

74

engineer shouting to the stokers. Then came a grinding sound as the giant spout was drawn out from the water tower and the rush of water as it filled the tanks on the train. All the while came the chuffing and gasping of the engine, just waiting to get going again, like a stallion biting at the bit. Luke picked up the impatience himself, ready now for the rush and the clamber and the adventure to begin.

"Hold it!" came a shout from below.

The rush of water ceased, and the rasp of rusty metal against metal, like giant fingernails scratching a blackboard as big as a mesa, let them know the water stop was about over. Frankie quick popped her head up, jerked it back and forth, and then plopped it down against the earth again. She was so close to Luke he could smell the milk from breakfast on her breath as she spoke.

"You ready?"

His cheek scratched the ground as he nodded.

"Let's go then."

She was up and running low to the ground, and Luke followed her down the dusty hillock just as the train was pulling out. Frankie cut a path at an angle ahead of the last car and Luke was right in her footsteps. She made a leap onto the metal ladder just in back of the rear wheels and scrambled up it like a monkey at the circus.

It looked so easy, Luke almost missed it. He made a leap but didn't allow for the movement of the train. His body slammed against the side of the car, and he held on for all he was worth. The train gathered speed, and looking down, he saw the gravel at trackside turning into a blur of movement. Still he held on, but he couldn't bring his body back level with the ladder. It was like he was sagging in the middle, his feet on the bottom rung and his hands clasped four rungs above that. The train was moving now, sailing along, and his hands began to cramp up. He felt paralyzed there smack against the side of that car, the wind blowing in his face as they clickety-clacked over a metal bridge crossing an arroyo. He couldn't even think, but he knew he could not hold on much longer.

There was no panic, no time for it. Suddenly there was something secure, something gripping him. He looked up and saw Frankie lying over the top edge of the car, grabbing his wrist and tugging at him until she brought him parallel with the ladder. He hugged its metal railings for a moment, breathing hard; then he scrambled up and over the top with her. The wind was fierce up here, blowing whatever words she was yelling at him back out into the arroyo behind them. He just nodded at whatever she was saying, thinking only that they had to do this all over again to get back to the ranch later today.

That thought ruined the great adventure of train travel for him. He should have followed his instincts, he knew, should have said no back at the ranch when Frankie had suggested it, should have just done his chores like he'd promised Pa and then done his homework and read some more. A nice peaceful Sunday.

She was up in a crouch, making her way forward on the train. He hadn't reckoned on this, that they'd actually be moving as the train was screaming along. She looked back at him, the wind blowing her blond hair all around her face, gave him a wave to follow, and he did. It was automatic. No thought. If he'd been thinking, he would've stayed hunkered down on the top of that flatcar until the next stop and then jumped off. But he followed, his thighs aching as he made his way, crouched down low against the wind. He held his arms out from his body like he was on a high wire, and the jiggling of the car made him lose his balance a couple of times until he finally reached the middle of the car.

Frankie had disappeared, but looking over the side, he saw that she had pried open the doors and swung down inside. She was looking up at him now, with something like fear in her eyes, but all he could do was just gape at her like she was crazy. He figured he was supposed to hang over the car feet first and swing in through the open car doors.

He shook his head at her. Maybe he was dumb, but he sure wasn't stupid.

Suddenly a large hand shot out of the car, grabbing his arm, and he was pulled off the roof of the car, dangling in space for a moment, and slammed to the wooden floor inside the car. The air was knocked out of him, and for a minute he couldn't move, could hardly breathe. When he looked up, all he saw was a pair of brown boots. And when he followed these up, he passed some khaki riding breeches bulging at the thighs, a Sam Browne belt, more khaki of a shirt, and finally a face atop it all, red and angry like freshly chopped meat. Two pinpoint eyes glared out at him from piggy features.

"What the hell you kids up to? You spies?"

He held Frankie in one hand, and she was struggling and wriggling around. But Luke could see the beefy hand holding her was strong enough that she wasn't going anywhere—the same hand that had hauled him off the roof.

"We're no damn spies," she yelped at him. "Just let me go."

She hauled off and kicked him. If he hadn't turned a half step, she would've got him where it hurts, too, but as it was, the kick landed on his thigh.

"No one ever teach you manners?" He brought his left hand around fast. She never even saw it coming. He slapped her so hard she landed on her back next to some wooden crates and tarpaulin-covered machinery.

Luke was up and jumped on the man's back. He could

77

feel how massive the man was as he gripped his neck, feel the ripple of muscle beneath him like horseflesh. The man shucked him off like a wet dog shaking water, and he landed on his back next to Frankie.

"You just lay there, the both of you. Not a move out of you, or I'll give you both the hiding of your lives. Bunch of rotten miner kids."

"We're not miners," Luke said, but Frankie put her hand on his arm to shut him up. He looked at her. Her cheek was red, and a trickle of blood showed in the corner of her lips.

"We'll see about that," the man said, then sat down on one of the big crates, his thick legs dangling over the side.

They did as he said, just lay there, not saying a word. Luke could see that Frankie was mighty curious about the tarped machinery, sort of inspecting it on the sly when the soldier wasn't watching them. Finally the train began to slow, and the soldier hopped off the box and went to the door, looking out at the terrain.

"That'll be Ludlow. We'll see about you kids there."

Frankie and Luke glanced at each other, neither saying a word, and the train stopped completely. The soldier swung around.

"Let's go." He grabbed both of them, and Frankie was not struggling now. They stood in the doorway of the platform at Ludlow near where Luke had been standing just yesterday, putting Beth on the train to Denver. The soldier looked around the platform, saw another couple of guys dressed in khakis, and called to them. One of them was tall and wore a peaked cap with a bright brass bar on it. He left the other militiaman and came up to the car.

The soldier holding Frankie and Luke looked flustered for a moment, then released Luke and saluted.

"Sorry, Captain," he said to peaked cap. "But I caught these two brats hopping the train. Come to spy for sure."

"We're not spies!" Frankie again protested.

The captain's eyes went back and forth between Frankie and Luke and then up at the beefy soldier.

"Good work." His eyes traced the man's sleeve for rank, for some identification. "Lieutenant . . . ?"

"Linderfelt, sir. I'm with Chase's company."

The captain nodded at this like it meant something. Luke thought he caught a slight smile on the man's lips.

"Spies, eh? Well, we'll deal with them here, Lieutenant. You may hand your prisoners over."

At which statement Linderfelt swung both Frankie and Luke out of the car, to land on the platform next to the captain.

"Watch out for the blond one. He kicks and got a mouth on him, too."

The captain looked at Frankie, at the bruise on her cheek, and then back to Linderfelt.

"Looks like there was an accident."

Lieutenant Linderfelt shook his head. "Fell getting into the car, sir."

"He hit me," Frankie spat out.

The captain surveyed them again with eyes like a vet's examining for broken bones. There was something easy and quiet in his manner that made Luke take to him. He wasn't the same as Linderfelt.

"That'll be all, Lieutenant. You reporting here?"

Linderfelt shook his head, glaring now at the captain, realizing that he was taking the kids' side. "No, *sir*," he said with an icy edge to his voice. "Headed for Walsenburg. Official business."

The captain nodded some more, chewing on his lips as if he was thinking. Then he breathed out hard through his nostrils like he made up his mind. The whistle sounded. The train was ready to pull out.

"We'll see to them, Lieutenant. Good day to you."

Linderfelt saluted, but it seemed more like a tip of the hat, and his little piggy eyes were flashing. The train pulled out, and Linderfelt stayed in the door watching them.

The captain turned to Luke and Frankie. "So what am I going to do with you two?"

"We're not spies, Captain," Luke said. "We were just trying to hitch a ride."

The captain's face lit up at this. He was young and fair-complexioned, and smiling, he looked not much older than Miss Nielson, their schoolteacher.

"Hobos, is it?"

"We're not hobos, either," Frankie said. "We got a home."

"No," the captain said. "I don't suppose you are. Friend Linderfelt does not seem to be the analytical type. Couldn't even tell that you're a girl, not a boy." He smiled at Frankie, but she wasn't being bought that cheap and returned his grin with a scowl.

"You belong here?" the captain asked, nodding toward the tent colony of strikers.

Luke shook his head. "We got a ranch just south of here. Pa does dairy runs."

An elbow in the ribs from Frankie told him he was talking too much.

"Why, Luke," a voice called to him from down the platform. He saw a shock of red hair. Mary Thomas was bustling toward them.

"What're you kids doing here on your own?" Then she noticed the captain. "Is there any trouble?"

The captain shook his head. "Not now." His eyes brightened at Mary Thomas and he must've liked what he saw, Luke figured, because he just kept on gaping until finally he blinked himself back to life. "Sorry," the captain said, taking off his cap. His light brown hair was ruffled in

80

the wind, and he had to scoop it back with his hand. "Captain van Cise, ma'am. You know these children?"

"Why, of course I do. They're from the Hayes ranch." She put a little straw shopping basket she was carrying down on the platform and placed an arm around each of their shoulders.

"That's good, then." The captain smiled. "I think they might've gotten lost or left out of their way. Maybe you could see they get home safely?"

"Of course." A squeeze from Mary Thomas for both of them.

The captain's eyes stayed fixed on Mary Thomas for a moment longer, like he was caught in a dream or listening to some pleasing music.

"Well, then," he said, catching himself staring again. "I guess I can be about my business." He put his peaked cap back on and lifted his arm as if to salute, then grinned again sheepishly and just nodded instead. Moving off lightly down the platform, he called out to the other soldier, "Sergeant, you get those notices up?" And then they were gone.

11

At the camp, Mary Thomas gave them both hot cups of tea in her warm little tent parlor with all the lace and doilies. Her two daughters were coloring at the table, giggling to themselves at the visitors.

Mary Thomas was at the stove, putting in freshly kneaded loaves of bread. She looked over her shoulder at Frankie.

"They tell me you play the piano."

Frankie looked down at her tea. "Some."

"Some?" Luke said. "She plays great, Mrs. Thomas."

Frankie shot him a mean look at this.

"Well, you do," he said.

"Ragtime and all, I hear," Mary Thomas said, wiping at a bit of flour on her cheek with her sleeve. "Wherever did you learn?"

Luke held his breath. No telling what she'd say to Mrs. Thomas. The way she hated people getting nosy, she'd most likely tell her to mind her own business.

But Frankie just smiled pleasantly. "I played in the cinema. They paid pretty good."

"Did you, dear? You mean accompanying the silent movies and all?"

Frankie nodded her head, then threw back the remaining bit of tea in her cup, shooting Luke a smile as she did so.

Was this before or after the poorhouse? he wanted to ask, but figured it wasn't worth the grief. Let her tell whatever stories she needs to, he told himself.

"Sounds like you've done some interesting things in your young life," Mrs. Thomas said, coming over to the table and joining them.

"Piano playing's easy," Frankie said. "Easier than most work."

"You'll have to play for us sometime at the camp," Mrs. Thomas said. "I'll sing with you." She put her hand on Frankie's, and to Luke's surprise, Frankie did not draw hers away.

Suddenly Frankie looked square at Mrs. Thomas and said, "I got to see Tikas."

"Whatever for, child?"

Frankie just shrugged. "Something he should know."

"Well, I'm afraid it'll have to wait. He's up in Denver for a few days. Getting his citizenship papers."

From outside came loud, angry voices; a shout that sounded maybe like someone's name but that Luke could not make out; and then a gunshot. Mary Thomas said not a word, but immediately bent over and pulled a carpet aside to reveal a trapdoor. She lifted this with surprising ease for being such a little woman and there was a hidey-hole under the floorboards of the tent. Her kids obviously knew what to do, for without a word they scurried underground. Another shot sounded from outside, making Luke cringe.

"Quick," she said to Frankie. "Get in."

Luke looked at Frankie, and her eyes seemed as big as the saucers under the teacups in front of them. She shook her head at Mary Thomas.

"Get down there," the lady said again. "It's the only safe place."

"I can't," Frankie finally said. "Can't stand tight places."

She just kept shaking her head and finally Luke took a peak out the tent flap and saw what the commotion was all about.

"It's all right," he said. "Looks like your men got things under control."

Mary went to the tent flap, leaving the trapdoor open, and her two little girls popped their heads out.

"It's okay now," Frankie told them. "Nothing to worry about."

They followed Mary Thomas out to where a crowd had gathered near the main tent. It seemed a couple of miners had gotten too much wine under their belts. One Greek and the other Italian. Taking target practice at some tin cans they tossed in the air. Tikas's second-in-command, a big, tough-looking Italian named Luigi, had them both by their collars now and was talking pretty fast and hard. Another Greek was trying to translate all this for the one in trouble, but he was looking pretty dazed. Luke figured maybe Luigi had knocked their heads together before starting to talk to them.

The upshot was that the two got extra cleanup duty as punishment and had their guns confiscated. The crowd of men, women, and children broke up then. Luke gazed out across the tracks and up the little rise where the National Guard units were encamped. Looked like full alert up there, rows of khaki-clad soldiers, arms at the ready, peering down at the camp. Smack in the middle of the soldiers stood the tall captain, field glasses to his eyes.

Luke wasn't the only one to notice. Luigi stood by him now, looking at the guard camp.

"Shooting down here," he said, "makes those boys nervous."

Mary Thomas had gathered her little girls into the folds of her skirt. Frankie stood by them.

"When's Tikas coming back?" Mary asked Luigi.

The big man shrugged. "When he gets here."

"Some of our men wouldn't mind a provocation," she said, fixing him with her gray eyes. "Besides, I thought all the guns had been confiscated."

Luigi shrugged again. "It's a strike, Mrs. Thomas. Strikes get violent."

"Not with the children here it won't." She flashed her eyes at Luigi, but he wasn't impressed.

"Those soldiers up there come to kill us. Maybe we should kill them first. That's what some say."

"We met the captain," Luke blurted out. "He seemed like a nice guy."

But Luigi wasn't listening to kids any more than he was to women.

"They come to fight, we give them a fight, whether Tikas wants it or not." And he stomped away before anything more could be said.

Mary Thomas watched him go, shaking her head at him. "Fool" was all she said. "Well, let's get you two kids home before your daddy finds you missing and worries half to death."

She managed to round up a buckboard, and the young kid Luke met before, Frank Snyder, was the driver.

"Hey, Luke," he said.

"Howdy, Frank. You know how to drive this thing?"

"Just like doing math tables." He'd put on some weight since Luke had last seen him, but still he wasn't what you'd call sturdy. And the pair of horses harnessed to the wagon weren't racing nags, either.

Luke climbed up and gave Frankie a hand, the three of them sitting together on the front board.

"This here's Francine," Luke said.

"Frankie."

"Yeah, well," Luke said, "this guy's Frank, and you're Frankie. There could be some confusion."

"I'm older," Frankie said.

"Not much in a name, anyway," Frank said, clucking at the horses and snapping the reins to get going. "Never cared much for mine. Always wanted to be called Vincent. That's a pretty good name, don't you think? Vincent."

He said it dreamily, like he was conjuring up foreign lands and fancy food.

"Heck of a name," Frankie said, but Luke could hear the bite in her voice and gave her an elbow in the ribs, which she immediately returned.

They pulled out of camp and onto the main road.

"How'd you guys get to the camp?" Frank asked, unaware of their scuffle.

And so they ended up telling him their adventures on the train and being caught by Linderfelt.

"Big fat guy?" Frank asked. "Like a pig bound for bacon?"

"That's the one," Luke said.

Frank shook his head. "You were lucky all he did was slap you. He's mean as mud."

Luke thought Frank was right. Linderfelt made even Sheriff Farr seem friendly by comparison. They rode in silence for a time. Frank was careful with the horses and confident. More like a man than a boy. They turned off the main road just past the Greens', and now, on the level stretch, Frank let the reins out a bit, the horses started to gallop, and they were jostled back and forth on the bench the next mile to the ranch.

"Nice of you to drive us back," Luke said after they arrived and he'd jumped down from the buckboard.

"That's okay," Frank said. "Nice to get out of the camp for a bit. See you soon, huh?"

"Sure," Luke said.

" 'Bye, Vincent." Frankie waved at the departing wagon.

They had got home before Pa at any rate, Luke could see. As they were walking to the house, he remembered something.

"So how come you wanted to see Tikas?"

"No reason. I don't want to now, anyway. It was stupid."

"Come on," he said. "Tell."

"Not worth telling, I guess, now I think about it," Frankie said. "But in that train car under those tarps—"

"I *thought* you were awfully interested in them," Luke said.

"Yeah." She was silent for a moment.

"Well?"

"You going to let me tell this or you want to?"

He reddened. "Okay. Go on."

"So under those tarps was a Gatling gun. That's what. And that clown guarding it, he's Chase's man, right?"

"Who's Chase?"

Another withering look from Frankie. "Don't you listen to your dad at all? He was talking about him just the other day. That puffed-up eye doctor they got running the guards. 'General' Chase. And he's not real neutral. Your dad says CFI cars are always parked outside his headquarters in Trinidad."

Luke wondered why he hadn't heard this. It was just that when Pa got that preachy voice on, he could hardly listen. His mind went wandering out to the pastureland, imagining hawks overhead or cattle grazing.

"Mr. Tikas needs to hear that," Luke said. "Maybe they're planning an action up in Walsenburg."

"Maybe they are, maybe they aren't. And maybe the miners are planning to shoot all the guards in their sleep.

87

It's stupid. All of it. Both sides. Both ready to kill for some words."

"It's more than words," Luke protested.

She just shook her head. "It's stupid. The ones with the most guns and money always win anyway. Besides, you think those strikers are all angels like Mrs. Thomas?"

He didn't reply to this.

"Well, they aren't." She answered her own question. "That Luigi is as much of a clown as Linderfelt. And those drunks shooting up the place could've killed a little kid easy. Bullets go up, they got to come down someplace."

She waited for him to respond, but he kept quiet. Her words were sinking in, though. He knew what she meant. There were good strikers and bad strikers, just like there were good mine owners and bad ones. Realizing that made it harder to act, harder to take sides. He felt sudden irritation at this complication she was bringing into his life.

"Let them kill each other, I say," she concluded.

"Tell me," he said, "how'd you know it was a Gatling gun under those tarps?"

"I could see it, you idiot."

"No. I mean, how come you know about Gatling guns at all?"

She didn't answer this, just shrugged her shoulders.

They got to the chores as quick as they could. Frankie helped him with skimming the cream in the barn. It reminded him of the night Beth killed the cat, and this memory blended with the multitude of events of the day, making him almost dizzy.

"Nice relaxing Sunday, huh?" he finally said into the silence between them. He wanted to call a truce.

This brought a small grin from Frankie and emboldened him.

"Was that true, that bit about playing at the movies?"

Frankie set the ladle down. "Why? Didn't it sound true?"

"That's not what I asked. Everything sounds sort of true from you. Even the bit about you being the poor little orphan who ran away from home. But I saw the play those lines are from. That's how come I knew you were telling stories."

She started skimming again. No response. The cows in the fields were beginning to call; time to bring them in soon. Luke knew that they'd have to hurry with the creaming if they wanted to get the cows in before Pa got home. But suddenly none of that mattered to Luke. Only the truth did. He was tired of pussyfooting around it.

"Look," he said as they finished skimming the last bucket. "I'm sorry about those welts on your back. I figure you showed me them to shut me up. To stop me prying. But I need to know, okay? I mean, it's not fair. You know everything about me by just being here. This is where I come from; this is what I do every day. But I don't know nothing about you. Not where you come from or what you did there or who your parents are."

"Were," Frankie suddenly corrected him. "I don't have any parents anymore."

She said this with a dead fierceness to her voice that made Luke want to believe that part.

"So, okay. You're an orphan. You really come from New York?"

"It's just none of your business, Luke."

"It is so."

"Why? You don't own me. Friends don't stick their noses in where they don't belong."

He desperately wanted to tell her that he wasn't just her friend, that he felt real love for her. Suddenly it was very

89

clear to Luke. The gnawing in his guts that he'd been feeling was love. That speeding of pulse when she was around, the wanting to please her even to the point of almost getting killed on the train today. It was a rotten trick, but that was the nub of it. He loved her.

But he didn't tell her any of that. "Friends don't lie to friends either," he said instead. "What we did together today, that's like a bond. That sack of cow dung Linderfelt could've hurt us. We were in it together. Don't you get it? There shouldn't be secrets if we're real friends."

"How many more scars do you need to see?"

He was about to protest, then realized she wasn't being literal. The scars she was talking about were not on her flesh.

"No," she finally said, "I don't come from New York, all right? I'm from Denver. And the closest I ever got to rich people was when my ma cleaned house for the Porterfields up on the hill." Her breathing came fast and her nostrils were flaring with each word, but she wasn't going to stop.

"Yes, I played piano at the movies, to earn just enough money to give to my dad so's he could go out and get drunk and then come home blind and mean as a snake and beat the living bejesus out of me and Ma. Is that what you wanted to hear? And that's where I learned about Gatling guns and all sorts of other things. At the picture palace. Those movies and that piano were about the best part of my life, 'cause at home, my dad would stick me in a tiny linen closet for hours and hours just for hollering out when he was beating me. Dark and cramped and full of scurrying noises and that's why I couldn't go down in that hole in the ground at Mrs. Thomas's."

She was crying now, and Luke wanted to tell her to stop, that it was okay. None of it was important.

"Is that the sort of information you want? How much more you need?"

He was about to reach out to her, to hold her in his arms like a crying baby, but she ran out of the barn and into the house, locking herself in her room. She didn't even come out for dinner. Luke told Pa that she was sick; she'd caught a chill out doing chores.

In a way, it was the truth. Luke was becoming an expert at half truths.

12

Ma returned the next day, and things went pretty much back to normal. Frankie didn't say anything more to Luke about the welts on her back or about her life in Denver, and he didn't ask. They had come to an understanding that didn't need words, and they both realized it. It was more than a truce, for Luke anyway.

With Beth out of the house, Ma now treated Frankie like everybody else. No more of the little waif tucked into her ample lap. Ma suddenly turned her no-nonsense switch on, and it was a relief to everybody. No more special treatment, no more "poor little Frankie" this and "darling little Francine" that. Partly it was because that was the way Ma treated her kids; partly, Luke now knew, it was because Ma was feeling bad about Beth. Those scars on Frankie's back explained a lot, explained why Ma was so protective of Frankie, why it looked like she was choosing a stranger over her own flesh and blood. Beth would be okay in Denver, mad as a smoked-out wasp, but basically okay. Frankie, however, was in danger. It was that simple.

Beth wrote regularly from Denver. At first the letters were all the same: a description of her daily routine and then a polite "I miss you" at the end. But after a while, she started talking about the museum and the theater and used words like *divine* and *adorable*, words she'd never use on her own, Luke knew. He could just see their aunt prompting her with what to say to the poor country folk back home. Luke could tell Beth was unhappy in spite of all the "divine" places Aunt Polly was taking her, and he felt bad about it, but it wouldn't be forever. Just a couple months, Ma said, until things settled down.

The next weeks were some of the happiest of Luke's life. Pa would drop Frankie and him off at school weekdays, and they'd act like they didn't know each other all day long. But he'd watch her when she wasn't looking. See her lips work as she formed the words she was beginning to read, observe the concentration on her wrinkled brow when she was doing sums on her slate board. The other kids let her alone. She didn't have any real friends, but then she didn't need any, Luke thought. He was her friend.

But she was like an older sister to the little kids she sat with, helping them to tie a shoe or pin up their hair when it got messed during recess. She never said anything about it, but it was like she was used to taking over. Playing big sister gave her a place in the school, and Miss Nielson took to her, you could tell. She was always giving Frankie special attention with her writing, leaning over her at the little table where she worked and laughing with her.

Pa would finally pick them up after his afternoon milk run, and Luke got to sit by Frankie all the way home, feeling the warmth of her next to him. The rest of the day they were inseparable. They did the outside chores together, helped to set the table and clear away afterward, and worked together on their schoolwork. Luke helped her with learning to read, and Frankie returned the favor by helping him with math. She had a natural head for numbers. It didn't take any schooling for her to be able to figure out pesky word problems about how many cups would fill three gallons or how many hours a train would take to reach New York City if it traveled thirty miles an hour.

They would sit at the kitchen table by the soft light of

the overhead kerosene lamp, their heads almost touching. Anything—the scratch of pencil on ruled and grainy tablet paper, the shuffle of book pages, the scuff of a chair edged in closer to the table—made him feel like he did after a long walk over pastureland. He felt the sort of peace and ease that being out in the big night under a sky chock full of stars gave him. Looking at her sometimes was like looking at a mess of those stars that suddenly focused into constellations. He couldn't put words to it.

There was peace in the coalfields, too. Pa was talking of the strike being over soon, and Luke was pleased about that. He'd sent a note to Louis Tikas with Pa, a message telling about the Gatling gun, and Tikas had written back a short thanks signed "Louis Tikas, U.S. Citizen." But the gun wasn't used. Both sides had settled down some. The Ludlow camp was still busting at the seams, but Tikas had managed to calm the men. It helped that most of the National Guard troops sent in were just regular guys; weekend warriors, Pa called them. They were workingmen with families, and they understood that you had to make a working wage. The mines were still operating, but lots of the scabs ended up at the Ludlow camp once they learned they'd been brought in to break a strike. Heck, there were even baseball games between the National Guard troops under Captain van Cise and the men at Ludlow. You can't play baseball with a guy one day and shoot him the next, Luke figured.

The weather held cold but fairly dry through November and into early December, but then one night Luke went to bed to a regular world and woke up in the morning to the strangest light he'd ever seen. It was like the world was on fire or something. He rubbed the sleep from his eyes and padded barefoot over to his window, wiping away the condensation. What he saw made him smile so wide that his scalp tightened.

It had snowed during the night. But not just any snow-fall. This one was like out of those Courier and Ives litho-graphs Ma would put up as decoration at Christmas, with big old dray horses pulling sleighs through mounds of chalky white snow. Outside, the snow was piled several feet deep and still falling. There were loaves of bread on the eaves of the barn, cotton wool over the pastures. A sudden ray of sunlight had broken through the cloud cover and was reflecting and glistening off the snow, and that was what caused the burning light.

He blinked a couple of times, not really trusting his eyes, and one thought played through his mind:

No school today.

The snow lasted on until Christmas, and at one point Pa, Luke, and Frankie got the sled out of the barn, hitched up the horse, and headed on over to Ludlow to help dig the strikers out. Their tents would collapse if the snow gath-ered on them, and even the guardsmen under Captain van Cise were in the camp helping to clear the snow. Luke ran into Frank Snyder again at the camp, and they shoveled snow for a time, shoulder to shoulder. Frankie headed for Mary Thomas's tent to be with the kids. There was a good feeling about it all, helping out and everybody being in it together. Like real neighbors.

Then came Christmas and Louis Tikas sent over an invite to join the camp at their festivities on the twenty-fourth.

"Be impolite to turn them down," Pa said.

"Of course we won't turn them down, Jethro," Ma said. "But you kids have got to dress warm."

Luke was amazed. He'd been sure Ma would say no.

Maybe it was the fact that Beth was staying on at Aunt Polly's for Christmas. She wrote that there was going to be a performance of *The Nutcracker* and she just couldn't miss it. Ma acted like she was happy for Beth when she read the letter, but Luke could see the disappointment in her eyes. She liked to have lots of people around at the holidays, and Beth's empty chair at dinner was especially noticeable this time of year.

So they bundled up for the trip to Ludlow. The roads had been plowed, so they could take the truck, but there was no way they could all fit in the cab. Frankie and Luke volunteered to ride in back, and Ma made them wrap two scratchy blankets around them for the journey. It was clear and moonless. The stars filled the sky, and Luke found Orion low in the east, fixing on the constellation as they made their way out to the main road. It felt good being close to Frankie in the back of the truck. They didn't need to talk. It was just quiet and comfortable. She leaned up against him to block the wind.

They could see the lights from the camp a good half mile before Ludlow. As they got closer, they saw why: Torches had been lit all around the perimeter of the camp, and smack in the middle of the compound was a tree that looked like it had been growing there half a century. They didn't even try and decorate it, just put small torches in its branches.

Pa stopped the truck by the entrance, and Mary Thomas and several other women formed a greeting party.

"So glad you could all make it," she said to Pa. Ma was introduced, and you could see she was impressed with how tidy and pretty Mary Thomas was. Not like her idea of an "anarchist striker" at all. There was fiddle music coming from by the tree, and it looked like most of the camp was gathered there for the fun. The torches lit the place like a big old hall and helped to warm things up, too. There were refreshments in the main tent, hot punch and plenty of pies. Luke could see some of the men tipping the contents of pint bottles into their steaming mugs, but everybody was smiling and laughing. If they were drunk, it was a happy drunkenness and not a mean one.

Captain van Cise and his men had been invited, too. Luke could see him talking with Louis Tikas by the punch bowl. Van Cise kept his eye on Mary Thomas as she brought in new arrivals. Some of the other ranchers from the area came, and the Hollearans from the station, the parents and the daughter.

"Hey."

Frank Snyder was standing next to him, his hair freshly scrubbed.

"How you doing?" Luke asked.

"See any more of that Linderfelt guy?"

Luke didn't much want to talk about him tonight. He just shook his head.

"No more hopping trains for you, huh?"

"Been too busy for that," Luke said, watching all the activity in camp.

"Math tables, huh?" Frank joked.

"Yeah. Something like that."

"She your girlfriend?"

"Who you talking about?"

"The one rode home with you. Francine."

"She just lives with us. Ran away from home."

"Doesn't mean she's not your girl."

Luke turned to the younger kid. "What do you know about girlfriends anyway?"

"Not much, and that's the honest truth. Some nice girls here, though. Lots don't speak English. But nice, you know?"

They stood in silence for a while and the noise around them came in waves, building up and then crashing over them—the men talking, women laughing, little kids circling the tree and screaming for joy.

"Just to tell you," Frank said suddenly. "I heard that Linderfelt at the depot the other day talking to some other soldiers. Didn't even notice me around. But he was talking about you two, I'm pretty sure. About what he was going to do if he caught you snooping on the trains again."

Luke said nothing but felt his face go red.

"So it's a good thing you're not hopping trains anymore, huh? Francine either."

Luke didn't have much time to think about this, for he now heard piano chords and saw that Frankie was at the piano and that Mary Thomas was shoving sheet music at her. The first chords of "Noel" rang out. Mary Thomas started to sing, high and so sweet that it brought goose bumps out on Luke's neck. Soon they all joined in the chorus, and when that one was through, they brought on "Deck the Halls." It went on like that for ten more carols, until Luke's voice was about hoarse. He loved the music of Christmas, and singing the old songs cleaned the bad taste of Linderfelt out of his mouth and got him back in the holiday spirit.

Tikas put a stop to the singing for a time.

"How about some presents?" he shouted. "Before all our younger members get too tired."

Out came this guy in the red one-piece underwear they called a union suit with a big black belt around the waist and some drugstore cotton for the whiskers. He wasn't carrying any bag over his shoulder, though, but pushed a big old cart loaded with wrapped-up gifts. There was enough in the cart for every boy and girl at the camp, too. A doll for the girls and a slate tablet and chalk for the boys.

There was more singing then, and finally the fiddlers took over, brewing up some lively dancing music, and Captain van Cise, he just walked right up to Mary Thomas by the piano and took her hand and off they went dancing. The strikers watched them, silent for a time. The only couple dancing. Then Pa dragged Ma, protesting, out to dance and the silence broke and everybody found somebody to whirl around. Luke made himself stop thinking and second-guessing and hurried over to where Frankie was.

"I don't know how," she said when he asked her to dance.

"We're even, then. Let's just give her a try."

And they did. With so many people moving around the huge tree, there was no one to say if you were a good dancer or not. It wasn't about being good or graceful, anyway, Luke soon discovered. It was about holding her to you, about smelling the fragrance of her hair, about smiling until your cheeks ached.

They kept at it until midnight at least, until the musicians were as tired as the dancers. Finally Luke and his family piled into the truck for the trip back home. Now Orion was high overhead and the polar star twinkled at them as they bounced over the rough road. Luke wondered how long such a perfect moment could last. How long such peace and warmth and love would be with them.

13

About three weeks later, Mother Jones came back to Trinidad, had a ham and egg breakfast at the Toltec Hotel, and got herself put into "protective custody," as General Chase, head of the National Guard troops in the region, called it.

"They've thrown her into jail," Pa told Luke. No double-talk for him. "Don't want her getting the boys all worked up. Looks like they were just stringing the union along. Paper says Governor Ammons himself ordered the arrest, and now they got the troops riding right along with the scabs, protecting them on their way to the mines. I guess they finally took sides."

Taking sides was exactly what Frankie did not want to do, Luke knew. She still thought the strike was a bunch of nonsense. Sure, she liked some of the people involved well enough, but *she* didn't want to get involved with it. No way.

The Trinidad paper for the week of January 20 split the Hayes household into two camps. On the front page was a warning by the editor, Forrest Hilyar, a buddy of the CFI boys, that there was to be a demonstration in town over the weekend, protesting the arrest of Mother Jones.

"Outside agitators from all over the state will be gathering in our fair city," Hilyar wrote in his front-page

100

editorial. "Anarchists and revolutionaries will descend upon us like locusts, yet, with the help of General Chase and his valiant National Guard troops, we shall prevail."

Pa threw the paper halfway across the room after reading the editorial out loud that evening, but Ma retrieved it. The back page drew her attention. Kincaid's was having a white sale to beat all white sales, so the ad told them. All fabric was on sale at half price.

"One day only," Ma said, sounding just like some kind of advertisement herself. "I've got to get to town this Saturday."

Luke and Frankie sat at the kitchen table, finishing some math problems and half listening to the voices in the front room at the same time.

"Don't you hear so good anymore, Anne?" Pa said. "Hilyar might be an ignoramus, but he usually gets his dates right. There's a big demonstration in Trinidad this weekend. I figure you don't want any part of that."

"That's right, Jethro." Ma's voice had that calm, slow sound to it that let Luke know she was getting ready for battle. "I don't want any part of that and I *won't* have any part of that. What I want is some calico for dresses and some bright print for new curtains in here. That's what I'm going to town for, and that's what I'm going to get."

End of conversation. Luke could hear the clicking of her knitting needles again.

"I think we're going to town this Saturday," he whispered to Frankie.

And so they did. It was a bright day with an uncommon warmth in the air. Pa dropped them off on Commercial Street. He had business with a cattle breeder just south of town. They would meet up again in the afternoon in front of the post office. Baruch, the notary, had an office there

101

and worked Saturdays, and Pa needed his services on some deeded land. So anyway, Ma, Luke and Frankie were left to the shopping. Luke didn't even ask if Pa wanted him along. He'd been to the breeders before. Not a pretty sight.

The town was hopping with people. There'd been trains coming in all morning, filled with women from the entire state. It was like some big fair or something. People were walking around town with smiles on their faces, enjoying the warmth of the sun, but also enjoying each other.

"Anarchists my foot," Ma said as they approached Kincaid's. "They're just a bunch of women."

Hearing the way she said it, you'd almost think she sympathized. But to nip any such thoughts in the bud, she added:

"Mind you, I don't hold with rabble-rousing. That Mother Jones or whatever her name is shouldn't be in custody, but she shouldn't be out here causing trouble either. Should be home dandling her grandchildren on her knee at her age."

Neither Frankie nor Luke bothered to respond. It wasn't the kind of statement that asked for a reply.

Kincaid's was as busy as the streets outside, but Luke could never remember being there when it was not. Payment and receipt cannisters were sliding along their cables up to and back down from the mezzanine, and Luke couldn't help but duck when he'd hear their whir along a cable. He also kept his eyes close on Frankie, but she wasn't in the mood for stealing today, not with Ma along, anyway.

Now, most people set free in a big emporium like Kincaid's would take about ten, fifteen minutes just to get oriented. Then there'd be another half hour picking through the merchandise they hadn't even known they needed or wanted before they set foot inside the store. By the time

102

they finally got down to what they'd come to town for, a good hour would be dead. Then came the hard decisions of how much to buy. Another half hour? Easy.

Not Ma. They were out of there in ten minutes flat, and two of those were spent waiting in line at the cashiers.

Both Luke and Frankie had their hands full carrying bolts of cloth and matching spools of thread.

"What're we going to do the rest of the day?" Luke said, blinking into the bright sun as they stood on the wooden sidewalk outside of Kincaid's.

"It's a fine day for walking," she said. "We'll leave these packages at Pa's notary; then we can maybe do a little window shopping."

She said it like a man might whisper a desire to sneak off to a saloon.

Just in the short time they had been in the store, the streets had seemed to fill even more with women and children. Luke read a banner one woman was carrying: HAS GOVERNOR AMMONS FORGOTTEN HE HAS A MOTHER? These women weren't organized yet, just milling around the streets, greeting one another, the kids holding on tight to their mothers' hands.

"Why don't we join the parade, Ma?" Luke winked at Frankie. He said it just to get a reaction.

Which he did. "Think they'd have something better to be doing on a Saturday than make fools of themselves."

They headed south down Commercial, Ma setting a furious pace and Frankie and Luke hurrying along in back of her as best they could with their bundles. At Main she turned left past the First National Bank and Masonic Temple, and finally they came to the post office. Things were a lot quieter on this end of town. According to the paper, the parade would end up at the county courthouse up the opposite end of Main Street.

103

Fred Baruch was in his notary office like always, and like always it smelled of old cigars. He was a short, bald-headed man in shirtsleeves, and he sat behind a roll-top desk, which completely obscured him from people coming into his office. You had to look for the trail of blue cigar smoke to find him. He was glad enough to take care of the packages until Pa came, but his face suddenly wrinkled with worry when Ma was getting ready to leave.

"You'll excuse me, Mrs. Hayes. None of my business, of course, but you haven't come to town to participate in the demonstration, have you?"

He had a pleasing but high voice and talked the way people did, Luke imagined, who had gone to college.

"Just shopping, Mr. Baruch."

His face brightened at that. "Good, then. There might be trouble, I've heard." He smiled at Luke and Frankie. "No use getting the children near that sort of thing, is there?"

"No, Mr. Baruch." Ma was never very warm with the man, but today she was cooler than usual, Luke noticed.

"Well, I'll look forward to Mr. Hayes's visit later today."

If he'd been wearing a hat, he would have doffed it. They left, Ma none too anxious to stick around the post office.

"Silly little man," she muttered as they were descending the front steps. "Can't see what he's—"

But she didn't finish her thought. Just to their left on Main Street was gathered a thick grouping of National Guard cavalry in their khaki tunics and breeches. General Chase himself, with his long white mustache, was wheeling his stallion in front of his men, pacing back and forth. The men looked tense, their eyes focused dead ahead of them, up Main Street.

Now Luke heard pipe music and the beating of a drum.

104

Frankie heard it as well, coming from their right. The cavalrymen were listening, and the ears on their horses were pricking up to it, too.

"What's going on?" Ma suddenly said.

"I think we'd better get out of here," Luke said.

But the three of them stood stock-still, not knowing which way to go.

The drums grew louder, and suddenly the procession of women and children turned into Main Street off of Commercial, the same way Luke, Frankie, and Ma had come only minutes earlier. There was a blood-red banner heading up the march: FREE MOTHER JONES.

"I thought they were supposed to go to the courthouse," Luke said.

"Me, too," said Frankie. "They turned the wrong way."

"Draw your sabers, men," Chase ordered.

Some nervous eyes were cast his way, but the men drew their sabers. Luke now noticed that one of the cavalry was none other than Linderfelt, the guy who caught them on the train.

The horses were now picking up the energy, stomping from foot to foot. The riders had a time keeping them in formation. Chase's stallion was getting edgy, as well, and it was all the general could do to keep him reined in.

Across the street Luke spotted a newspaperman with his camera in hand, snapping pictures of the parade. When he saw the cavalrymen all lined up with sabers at the ready, he started taking pictures of them.

"Ma." Luke touched her arm. "Maybe we better go back inside." It was the last thing he wanted to do, but it was what Pa would have suggested, he knew.

"Nonsense, boy. They're just women. The soldiers will send them off home with a good scolding."

He looked at Frankie, and she shook her head.

The parade kept coming on, and Chase on his horse paced back and forth in front of his men. The leader of the parade, a woman in blue hat and coat about Ma's age, halted some ten yards from the cavalry, the drums stopping in midbeat.

"We have a parade permit," she said. "We intend to pass."

Luke spotted Mary Thomas and her two little girls in the second row of the protesters. She was craning her neck around the woman in front of her, trying to get a look at what was going on.

"Your permit does not extend to this precinct," General Chase said in a voice so reedy as to be hardly heard above the snort of horses. "You well know Mother Jones is being held not far from here."

The leader smiled. "Do you think we are going to storm the Bastille, General?" Then she turned around to address the rest of the protesters. "Come on, ladies. Let's finish our parade."

The drum set up again and the women and children moved slowly forward. Chase didn't seem to know what to do. He just looked gruffly at them as they approached. A crowd of other onlookers had now gathered around the spectacle; there were shouts and jeers. Some for, some against. One of the first of the paraders to reach Chase was a young girl, not much older than Frankie. As she tried to edge around his horse, the general suddenly kicked at her with a stirruped boot, catching her square in the chest. Luke could not believe his eyes as the girl staggered back, hand to her chest. The onlookers booed. Someone tossed an apple at the general, and his skittish horse reared up and threw Chase off, to land flat on his back on the cobbled street. This brought a round of laughter from protesters and onlookers alike.

"Serves him right," Ma said.

But then General Chase struggled to his knees, looking bitterly at the protesters. "Ride down the women!" he shouted.

There was absolute silence for a moment. No one could believe he'd actually ordered it, not even his own men.

"You heard what I said. Ride them down!"

The cavalry hesitated a moment and then Linderfelt yelled, "Charge!" and suddenly the street was a mad and crazy broiling of horses and women. Linderfelt ripped the American flag out of the hands of a woman in the front row of protesters and got clubbed on the head with a banner for his trouble. Then came the flash of sabers. Luke found himself all but paralyzed as he saw a red streak of blood erupt on the forehead of the woman in blue. The woman beside her put her hands up to protect herself, and Linderfelt slashed at her hands with his saber. There were screams and frantic running in every direction.

The cavalry regrouped and now Chase was on his horse again, his pistol drawn, and he led the second charge even as the women were fleeing. Chase used his pistol like a club, swinging it right and left at women as his horse pounded into their midst.

Luke suddenly realized that Frankie was no longer at his side. He quickly pulled Ma back into the safety of the post office foyer.

"Stay here, Ma," he told her. "I'll be back in a minute. Don't move."

She could say nothing. The sight of those cavalrymen had shocked her into silence.

Back out on the street the cavalry was charging for a third time, and now Luke saw Frankie. She was helping Mary Thomas get her kids out of the way of the charging horses. Banners and posters were strewn over the street along with hats and here and there a shoe.

"Frankie!" he shouted. "Watch out!"

But it was too late. The general caught her on the back of her head with his pistol and she crumpled to the ground in the midst of the charge, the horses' shod hooves sparking against the cobbles.

14

Luke raced to Frankie in time to keep her head from getting squashed by the general's horse. By then Chase was on to better pickings, hammering at the women's backs as they tried to get to the safety of sidewalk and buildings. Luke lifted Frankie in his arms. She was out cold, breathing heavy like she was asleep, and he was thankful for that at least. He looked at his sleeve. There was blood where her head rested against his arm, more blood on the cobbles where the sabers had been at work.

Luke couldn't manage her in his arms, so he had to drape her over his shoulder, gently, but her head hung down loose. Couldn't be helped, though, and he actually found himself muttering an apology to Frankie as he stumbled across the street toward the post office. His way was blocked suddenly by a cavalryman, his horse lathered up and its eyes huge and terrified on each side of its giant head.

"Well, if it isn't the spy."

Linderfelt sat on the horse, grinning down at Luke, saber still in hand. There was a thin line of crimson on its blade.

"She's hurt" was all Luke could muster. No fear; he was too shocked for that. He should have been scared, though.

Linderfelt squinted hard at him, his horse pumping against the tight reins.

"No more than she deserves," he said.

"I got to get her some help." Luke tried to move around the horse, but Linderfelt wheeled in front of him. "She wasn't even in the parade," Luke shouted at him. "Let me by."

Linderfelt squared his shoulders, his fat lips pouted, his hand tensed on the saber.

"You've been asking for it from the get-go, haven't you now? Time you learned some respect."

His arm raised and the saber glinted in the sunlight.

"You put that pig sticker down."

It was a shriek of a command that hurt the ears. It caught Linderfelt so much by surprise that he twisted his head around this way and that. Luke ducked, turned, and saw Ma striding out into the middle of it all, her hat cock-eyed on her head, a strand of hair flopped down in her face. But her walk meant all business.

"You ought to be ashamed of yourself," she shouted at Linderfelt as she approached the horse and tucked a protective arm around Luke and the unconscious Frankie.

But that wasn't enough for Ma. "All of you," she said, wagging her head in disgust. "Ashamed! Your own mothers wouldn't claim you."

Linderfelt's openmouthed surprise was changing to anger. His face went red and his eyes bulged. Just as he was about to swing the saber, Chase came riding by.

"Let's round them up, Lieutenant," the general ordered. "The detainees will be held at the bank for now."

Then Chase looked down at Ma and Luke and Frankie. "You folks get along now. Shouldn't be here, anyway."

He turned his horse. Linderfelt stared at Luke like a bully on the playground.

"Make it quick, Lieutenant," Chase called, and Linderfelt reluctantly followed.

The crowd had spread out the length of Main Street

now, but the cavalry had concentrated on arresting only the leaders. Ma helped Luke with Frankie, and together they climbed the steps to the post office.

By the time Pa got to town, Frankie had come around. Pa held up a finger in front of her eyes and made her track it back and forth a couple of times, then pronounced her okay.

But Frankie was not all right. The first words she spoke to Luke once Ma and Pa were out of earshot were "I'm going to pay them back."

Luke hid his pleasure at this. Finally they were on the same side about the strike, he thought. Partners.

Turned out they arrested Mary Thomas *and* her kids, too. They all three made such a fuss, though—Mary Thomas singing Welsh songs all day and night and the kids making a mess out of the washroom—that Sheriff Farr let them go the next day. The rest of the women were held a couple more days and then sent on their way.

But the event was not forgotten. Local and state newspapers picked up the story: COSSACKS CHARGE INNOCENT WOMEN AND CHILDREN the headline from the Denver *Chronicle* screamed. Then the national papers got into the game, and soon the whole country was looking at the events in Trinidad. But that didn't help to get rid of Chase; it only made the miners madder than before and brought out the meanness in everyone.

"Just what Chase wants," Pa said one night about a week after the saber charge. "Have the boys come with rifles blasting so he can say they got a major insurrection going here, so he can call in the federal troops and squash the strike like a bug on the wall."

Ma was trying to concentrate on her knitting but not having much success. Finally she put her needles down.

"I can't understand why that man is still in charge. He

rode them down, Jethro. Women and kids. What kind of leader is that?"

"Chase says it was provoked," Pa answered. "The governor's leaving him in charge."

Luke was in the front room tonight, seated on the one long divan next to Frankie, acting like he was busy with schoolwork. But his ears were alert to the conversation instead.

"Provoked!" Ma slapped her thighs with open hands. "Why, he kicked a girl not older than Francine here, and then he fell off his horse. His pride was hurt. That's what provoked him."

"I'm not defending the man," Pa said, putting down the newspaper he was reading. "Just explaining. In fact, if the boys start using their rifles, I'm not so sure I wouldn't want to join them for what they did to Francine."

These words took the wind out of Ma's sails, changed her feisty to cautious.

"Now hold on, Jethro. It's their fight, after all. I'm just thankful little Beth is safe in Denver."

Frankie got special treatment at school, almost like a hero, after she got biffed on the head in Trinidad.

"How come they didn't arrest you?" Peter Brothers asked during morning break the first day Frankie went back to school.

"She was out cold," Luke said.

They wanted to see the bump at the back of her head and she obliged them, acting like she thought it was all stupid, but Luke could see that underneath she was pleased to be the center of attention for once.

"Weren't you scared?" Phil Small asked. "I mean they had swords and all."

"I was just trying to help Mrs. Thomas with her kids," Frankie told them. "Didn't have time to be scared."

"I would've shot him," Betty Carlson declared, but nobody was listening to her and she went off to the parallel bars to spin herself goofy.

Billy Wilder tried to act above it all.

"My father says they were headed for the Mount San Rafael Hospital. That they were going to let Mother Jones free. My father says she's the most dangerous woman in America now. The troops were just doing their duty."

Nobody bothered to reply to him, either. It sounded like a load of hog slop and even he knew it. Samuel Kincaid and he stood apart from the other kids for a while. But curiosity got the better of them, as well, and Billy whistled admiringly when he finally ran a finger over the lump on Frankie's head.

"Hurt?"

She looked at him with narrow eyes. "Yeah."

"Should keep ice on it," he said.

She smiled. "Thanks for the tip."

Luke felt a sharp pain like a stab in his chest, watching them making friends with each other.

"So I've got it figured out," Frankie told him that day after school. Milking time and he had his head against the warm side of one of the milk cows, his hands working rhythmically on the udder. The milk made a pinging sound as it squirted into the galvanized bucket underneath.

"What you got figured out?"

"How we're going to do it."

He stopped milking and turned to her. "Do what?"

"Get even."

He went back to milking, smiling at her use of *we*.

"You want to hear?"

"I'm listening," he said.

She looked over her shoulder. Pa was three stalls from them, milking. Far enough away he couldn't hear.

"We set her free."

It didn't mean anything to him at first. Set *who* free? Then it clicked. He stopped milking again, swiveling around on the little wooden stool to face Frankie.

"You must be crazy."

She shook her head. "Nope."

"You got a plan?"

"I'm working on it. I need to see the place first."

Luke thought about it for a while. He could just see Linderfelt's face when he got the news. It'd be worth it for that alone.

15

Their chance came the next Saturday. In all the rush and commotion the day Frankie got knocked out, Ma had forgotten the packages at Baruch's office. Pa needed to go visit the cattle breeder near Trinidad again, so Frankie and Luke took the trip to town with him.

Pa didn't know about the private war between Linderfelt and Frankie and Luke, else he would have thought twice about letting them hang around town for a while like they asked.

"You're going to turn into a city kid, you don't watch out," he joked with Luke when he dropped them off at the post office.

Same arrangement as usual: He'd pick them up at Baruch's in a couple hours.

They didn't waste any time but headed straight for the hospital where Mother Jones was being held. A big old building built of granite blocks, it looked more like a fortress than a hospital, set on a rise of ground just to the east of town. It didn't take a Baldwin–Felts detective to tell where Mother Jones was being kept. A guard stood outside a bottom-floor window, bayonet fixed to his rifle. Frankie and Luke took up position under a live oak across the street from the hospital. Through the vertical poles of a wrought-iron fence that surrounded the hospital grounds, they watched the militiaman smoke a cigarette, then squash it with his boot on the pebbled path, pick up his gun, and march back and forth under the window like some toy store mechanical soldier.

"Come on," Frankie said as she left the security of the tree and headed up the street.

Luke wanted to ask what she had in mind but decided he'd just let her lead things for a bit. Let her come out with it at her own pace. Partners trust each other.

She crossed the road once they were past the hospital and then turned down a side street in back of it. Not many buildings out here; the town pretty much ended with the hospital. One little white-painted house, a picket fence, and a dog that barked too loud at them. The sudden yapping made Luke tense up inside. Soon they reached the rear of the hospital. The iron fence continued around here. Some laundry hung on a line on the other side of the fence, but nobody seemed to be on duty.

"Give me a hand up," Frankie said, looking at the spiked top of the fence.

Luke's patience gave out. "What are we going to do?"

"*I'm* going to go over the fence and scout things out. *You're* going to wait here."

She said it with the kind of firmness to her voice that let him know there was no arguing. He just stood there for a moment, however, studying the fence, checking for guardsmen on the grounds.

"Move it," she commanded. "While the coast is clear."

He meshed his fingers together, forming a stirrup with his hands, and she put a foot in. Then he boosted her as high as he could. She grabbed on to the spikes of the iron fence, hefted a leg, and then pulled her body up to straddle the top horizontal bar. Another quick movement and she dropped to the ground on the other side, facing him.

"How you going to get back out?" he asked.

By the wide look of her eyes, Luke figured she hadn't thought of that one, either.

"Just wait here," she said, but there was a quaver in her voice now.

Not much else he could do but wait. Still nobody around, but he could hear voices from in front, the sound of a car driving up, its door opening and then slamming shut again. That dog was still yapping, too. The sound got on Luke's nerves. There were some bushes along the line of the fence, and he thought maybe it was a good idea to squat down behind these. Turned out to be a very good idea because the bushes partially hid a gate in the fence. He tried the handle; it turned. It was rusty and had obviously not been used in a good long time, but the gate opened once he put some weight behind it.

By the time Frankie got back from her scouting, he was standing just inside the fence with a grin on his face.

"I like doors," he said. "More civilized."

She didn't respond to this.

"Where they've got her," she said, "the whole wing is locked up. But you can get in the main part. There's still patients and nurses there. Catholic. They're all dressed in those."

She jabbed her thumb over her shoulder to a pair of nun's habits hanging on the line.

"The kitchen is back here, too," she continued, "and I eavesdropped for a bit on the cook and her helpers. Seems Mother Jones has her food delivered by the sisters. Doesn't trust the guards. Thinks they'll poison her food. They were having a good gab session about it."

She looked pleased with herself. "I think I got a plan."

When Luke got to the main hall, he saw the registration desk and the nurse in back of it. He tried to act calm; he put his hands in his coat pockets, looking as if he were waiting for someone. I'm here to see my aunt, he rehearsed, if anybody asked him. My ma's with her now. I'm just waiting.

He strolled down the hall behind the registration desk, and just as Frankie said, he found the fire alarm.

"Use only in the event of fire," the sign next to it said. "False alarms will be prosecuted."

He swallowed hard reading these words, then walked back out to the main hall, keeping his eyes peeled for Frankie. He looked up at the big pendulum clock on the wall: 12:02. Two minutes passed as he watched the pendulum swing back and forth in its glass case. Then five.

What if I missed her? he thought. What if she's already in there waiting for me to pull the alarm? I should've been quicker.

Finally he saw Frankie, dressed in a nun's habit, face down, a covered plate in her hands. She walked right by him without turning her head an inch his way. He watched her go to the locked door to Mother Jones's wing. The guard there unlocked the door, checked under the napkin to make sure she was bringing only food, then waved her on toward Mother Jones's room.

Luke began counting even as he moved to the alarm. Frankie had told him to give her a thirty count before pulling the alarm. Ten, eleven, twelve, he counted. He was at eighteen by the time he reached the alarm. He looked over his shoulder. A nurse came out of a door in front of him just as he was reaching for the alarm, and he quickly changed the destination of his hand to reach up and wipe at his nose. Twenty-two, twenty-three, he counted, waiting for the nurse to get on past.

He read the warning again: "False alarms will be prosecuted."

Twenty-eight, twenty-nine.

His mouth was dry and his hand was shaking as it reached out.

Thirty.

He shut down his mind, shut out everything as he gripped the lever. Before he knew what had happened, bells began ringing all over the place. He quickly moved away from the alarm, trying to act as surprised as everybody else.

"Fire!" the nurse at the main desk shouted, and the guard on duty at the entrance to the far wing unlocked his door to see what the commotion was all about.

"Fire!" the nurse yelled at him.

"Where?" he said, but his question was lost amid the general pandemonium of people trying to get out of the building.

Luke made his way upstream against the people running for the front doors. He put his shoulders sideways, was bumped and buffeted, but finally he got to the corridor leading to the back exit. The halls here were clear and he suddenly started racing, breathing through his mouth. It felt good to move like this, a relief to let himself go, and in a matter of seconds he was out the back door and running across the yard toward the rear gate. The others had left the building, but no one had stayed in the back. They had all filtered around to the front to see what was going on. In the distance he heard the bells from the fire station; trucks would be here soon.

Hurry, Frankie. Don't take all day.

But she didn't come.

He hunkered by the little gate in the fence for a while and still no Frankie. Finally he couldn't take it any longer. He knew it was dumb, but he had to go back in there and see what had happened. Maybe they caught Frankie. Maybe this, maybe that. Heck with it, he thought.

He got back into the main hall without anybody stopping him, and the door to Mother Jones's wing was open. He walked on down the hallway, hearing voices screaming outside to get the fire trucks up here, feeling his heart pumping in his chest so fast that he thought it'd pop.

A door was open to his left and, peeking in, he saw Frankie, still in the nun's outfit, and Mother Jones seated by the window, making no move to change clothes.

"What's going on?" Luke said, coming into the room. "We gotta get moving."

Frankie looked at Luke blankly. "She's not coming."

"This the young friend who's waiting for me?" Mother Jones said, a smile on her face.

"Not coming!" Luke shouted.

"Shh." Frankie held a forefinger to her lips.

"Not coming?" Luke said again, but almost in a whisper.

"No, son," Mother Jones said pleasantly, like she was turning down a second cup of coffee at breakfast. "As I was telling this brave young girl, I'm of more use inside than outside."

"But the miners need you," Luke pleaded.

Frankie said nothing, just stared out the window at the people running around outside.

"They've *got* me," Mother Jones said. "I'm much more valuable to them in here, locked up, a poor old woman jailed. In here I'm a martyr. I'm excellent copy for journalists." A soft, dry chuckle came from her. "Out there I'm afraid I'd just be a silly old lady on the run."

"The miners would hide you," Luke said. But they'd never thought that far ahead, never planned what to do once they got Mother Jones out.

"But I don't want to be hidden." She smiled at them. "Now you two take yourselves off out of here before the valiant guards return. Scoot, hear me?"

120

Luke didn't need to be told twice, but Frankie lingered in the room. Suddenly they heard footsteps outside the door, men coming back down the hall.

"Quick," Luke said to Frankie. "Give me that other outfit."

She was almost in a trance, it seemed, so that Luke had to reach into her habit and pull out the other set of nun's clothes, meant for Mother Jones. He slipped this habit on and wrapped the sort of kerchief affair low so it covered all his hair and went down over his forehead. The skirt reached to the floor, covering his boots.

"Let's go," he hissed at Frankie.

Mother Jones was enjoying this show.

"Thank you, sisters," she said loudly as the footsteps approached the door. "I'm fine here. It was good of you to check on me."

Just then a guard poked his head in the open door.

"What's this?" he said gruffly.

Mother Jones stood now, casting a fiery glance his way.

"These two brave sisters were checking to see that I was in no danger from the fire. It's more than you guards did, too busy saving your own behinds."

The man's face reddened. "There's no fire." He looked Luke and Frankie up and down. "False alarm."

"Then your worries were for nought," Mother Jones said, turning to the two of them. "But thank you again for caring. Now be off with you."

Luke pulled Frankie with him out of the door, forcing himself to walk slow and easy. They went out the back way again and luckily ran into no real nuns, who were mostly still gathered in the front. Out back in the bushes they shucked off the habits and then ran like Linderfelt himself was chasing them.

*   *   *

Pa picked them and Ma's bundles up as arranged at two o'clock.

"You kids have any fun?" he asked.

"We were looking in the shops," Luke said.

Pa grunted at this, putting the Mack truck into gear. "Heard the fire trucks were at the hospital today," he said, keeping his eyes straight ahead of him. "Somebody pulled a fire alarm up there. Sherriff Farr's mad as a wasp about it. Interrupted his lunch, I hear."

Luke and Frankie were silent as the truck rattled down Commercial and out of town.

Later that night the wind started up and rain came soon after. Luke went to her room once he was sure Ma and Pa were sleeping.

No answer to his light knock, so he just went in. The lamp was off, but he could tell she wasn't asleep. Her eyes, all white, were blinking in the darkness.

He went to her bed and sat down on the side, making the springs sound. The wind was building up to a good blow outside.

"So," he began, "we gave it a try."

She blinked once at him. Twice.

"Close one," he said. "I thought that guard had us sure."

More silence. "She's just like all the others," Frankie finally said, her voice low and without its usual sparkle and pop.

"What do you mean?"

"I mean what I said. Just like all the others. Working an angle. Everybody's got an angle."

Luke thought about this. "It sounded smart enough to me. She *is* a martyr in there."

"That's what I mean. It's smart. All planned out. Like

she wanted it this way from the beginning when she came back to Trinidad. She's got her angle. I thought she was different. That maybe she really cared. Really believed what she says. That she'd want to be rescued."

"Just because she plans things out doesn't mean she doesn't believe in what she does."

A snort came from Frankie. "That's what you say. I say she's working an angle, just like everybody else. Playing her cards close to her chest."

The rain battered against the window. They didn't speak for a time.

"So what's this mean?" Luke said. "You don't believe in the strike now?"

"Who says I ever did believe in it? And besides, what's to believe in? They're all the same. All playing the angles. There isn't anybody who just says the plain truth and then acts on it."

"How about Tikas?"

She laughed. "That Greek? He's out for himself just like all the rest."

"And Mary Thomas?" Luke felt anger rising like a temperature in him. "Is she just playing the angles, too?"

"She hasn't got any choice. She's stuck in it. Stuck with her kids and no husband. That's what you can't let happen to yourself. Getting stuck. Getting involved. They fooled me for a minute there, but Mother Jones wised me up. You look out for number one. You find your angle and then play it."

"It isn't all angles," he said, thinking for an instant of his brother, Tom, killed down the mine shaft. Blown into so many pieces they didn't know who they were burying.

"There's good reasons for a union," he said with real conviction.

"Sure. So's the union bosses can make a nice fat salary. So's a bunch of out-of-work soldiers got a job."

"Captain van Cise isn't like the others," he said, misunderstanding her.

"I don't mean the guards. I mean those Greeks at the tent camp. They've been fighting wars in their own country so long they don't know any other life. They're going to do it here, too. They're not miners. They're hired guns."

Luke shook his head. "What're you talking about?"

She sat up in bed now, pursing her lips. "Do I have to tell you there's no Santa Claus? Open your eyes, Luke. It's not all black and white like you think. Not all good or all bad. Tikas might be okay, but he's got a bunch of gun-happy men out there just itching for a big fight. Van Cise is okay, too, but once he leaves, guess who's in charge?"

"Linderfelt," Luke said.

"Right. And that's a nice recipe for disaster there. Linderfelt and the Greeks."

"So you just stay out of it altogether, is that it?" He wanted to get to her, to make *her* open her eyes.

"That's about the size of it." She scooted back down in bed now, pulling the covers up under her chin.

"And if everybody did that, nothing would change."

She snorted at this. "That's a good one. Change."

"You don't believe in change?"

"Oh, that's not a problem. Most things get worse before they get better."

"I mean good change."

She didn't reply, looking up at the ceiling instead.

"But it is possible," he said, believing it now for the first time. "So Mother Jones has got an angle. We've all got them. You had yours today. You wanted to free Mother Jones to get even, not to help her. But sometimes angles are for good reasons."

"It's easy for you to say," she suddenly hissed at him. "You were born where it's good."

"Oh, so that's it. The poor-little-girl act again. And you were born where it's bad, and ain't that too bad." He felt a knotting at his throat with the sudden anger. "And that's the way things'll always be for you if you believe it."

They said nothing for a time as the wind and rain whipped against the bedroom window.

"Okay," he finally said. "So I'm sorry. I haven't lived like you—"

"You don't even have an idea how I lived," she said, and her voice sounded a long way off and close to tears.

"And like Pa says," Luke went on, "I shouldn't make judgments. But it's good for you now, isn't it? It's good here with me, with us?"

"Like you say, things change."

"I won't." His anger suddenly drained from him, replaced by an ache for her, a wanting to protect her. "Not about you. Not ever."

She looked toward the window. There was a smile on her face, but her chin trembled.

16

There was a heavy snowfall the day they got the letter from Aunt Polly.

"It says Beth's sick," Ma declared after reading her sister's letter. "They don't know what it is."

Luke didn't like the tremor in Ma's voice as she related that information.

Next day, Ma and Pa went to the station to pick Beth up. Luke saw her after coming home from school. She was in her room, tucked under a snowdrift of covers, her little face as white as the sheets and her hair dull and straight against the pillow.

"Hey," Luke said, poking his head inside her door. "How you doing?"

She cast a poor excuse for a smile his way. "Okay."

He came in, taking that as an invite. "You don't look okay."

"Thanks."

"Where do you hurt?"

She gave a little shrug. "All over."

"Been having fun in Denver?" He didn't know what else to say, just hated seeing her so helpless.

"Not much," she said. "Been in bed lately. How's your friend?"

"Frankie? She's doing fine."

Beth just stared at him, not blinking. He looked away first.

"That's good," she finally said, but it came out sounding just the opposite.

Luke's heart sank. Beth was still filled with the same old spite even when she was laid up with some sickness.

"Jesus, Beth. Just let it go."

"So you're swearing now, too. That's her doing."

"I give up." He turned to go.

"You don't know about her, do you?"

This stopped him, but he didn't turn around to speak.

"Yeah, I know," he said to the door. "She told me."

"Everything?"

Turning, he saw that there was color in Beth's cheeks now, like she could feed off hate.

"I know she's not from New York but from Denver. And that her mother was a housecleaner, her dad some drunk who beat her. She's had it pretty rough, but that's not a crime. So can't we all just be friends?"

Beth shook her head, propped against the pillow. "She didn't tell you everything, did she? I knew she wouldn't. You want to hear?"

"No," he almost shouted and then left the room.

"What she tell you?" Frankie said as they were finishing evening chores.

"Nothing," Luke said as he closed the door to the cheese room.

Outside the barn, the snow was already melting, leaving patches of muddy brown.

"She told you something," Frankie insisted. "You're different."

They walked side by side back to the house.

"She didn't tell me anything," he said again, then stopped. "Why? Is there something to tell?"

Frankie stopped a step ahead of him and then slowly

turned. Her cheeks were red from the cold, and the vein at her forehead pulsed. Luke would never forget the look in her eyes at that moment. He didn't have the words for it, but it was a mixture of the way a horse will look at you when it's suspicious and scared and of the way a dog will when you're feeling low-down and take a swipe at him for no good reason.

"Things always change, don't they?" she said and then quickly turned and ran to the house.

Beth got better almost immediately. Doc Marlow from Tabasco said he'd never seen such a speedy recovery. Ma allowed that Beth had only been suffering from homesickness.

Luke almost succeeded in putting Beth's taunt out of his mind. He tried to make it up with Frankie, told her nothing had changed now that Beth was back, that Beth was just a pill. He almost believed it. And Frankie acted like it was okay, too, but Luke could tell it was an act. She was on guard now, kept things to herself. He'd find her out in the barn lying in the hay all on her own, just staring into the rafters. When he'd ask her what she was doing, she'd only shrug at him.

"Thinking," she'd say, chewing on a stick of straw. "Just thinking."

For weeks Luke picked at his scab of doubt until he couldn't take it any longer. It was early on a Sunday morning in March, and Beth did not sleep late like usual. She was up when Luke was getting ready for his chores. Ma and Pa were having a sleep in and Frankie never did the early milking, so it was just Luke and Beth.

"Poor Luke," Beth said, standing in the kitchen doorway. "Got to do the chores all alone this morning."

"Doesn't bother me," he said, gulping down the glass of

milk he'd poured. "It's what Pa does all the time. I'm the oldest."

She was still in her flannel nightgown with a maroon bathrobe over it wrapped up tight to her throat. With a smile, she left the door and sat at the table with him, but all he wanted to do was get outside to his chores. He could hear birdsong; it was warming up. A slanted ray of sun poured through the kitchen window and onto the table, lighting up a million dancing bits of dust.

"Maybe I should start helping with the milking again," she said.

"Maybe," Luke said. "When you get stronger."

Beth had not yet been back to school. Plans were for her to return tomorrow.

"It gets boring cooped up in here all day."

He smiled at this. She used to complain like a sore tooth about having to help with the chores. Not ladylike, she would say.

"Well, it does," she insisted.

He shoved his chair back from the table and stood. "Got to go. The cows are waiting."

"Luke." She was looking down at her hands in her lap.

And suddenly he'd had enough. He could feel something inside him breaking loose like a flooded arroyo.

"Okay," he said. "So what is it you know? Tell me and let's get it over with."

"You *should* know it," she said. "So should Ma."

"Out with it," he said, his hands clenched into fists.

She told him, told him plain and without any real happiness in the telling. He listened, even when he wanted to shove his hands over his ears and blot out her voice. Listened and the words hit at him, stung him.

"I don't believe you," he said after she'd finished.

"Ask Aunt Polly."

"Besides, it could be lots of people from that description."

She shook her head. "Someone who plays the piano like that? Someone just Frankie's age and height and weight?"

"Did Aunt Polly ever see her? Did she ever go to this Madam Floe's?"

"I heard them talking," Beth insisted. "It was Floe herself, all gussied up in a red gown in the middle of the day, with lipstick thick enough to choke on. She was sitting in Aunt Polly's parlor when they thought I was napping. Uncle Carl complains she always takes her social work home, even to meeting clients there. He says people in the neighborhood are beginning to wonder about the kinds of friends they keep. And so I heard Madam Floe, plain as day. How this young girl of hers ran away, this Françoise, she called her. That she thought maybe Aunt Polly or some other social worker got to her and took her away."

"So what does that prove?" The name jingled in his memory. Madam Floe's. He had heard it somewhere.

"It proves what kind of person she is," Beth said, her voice rising. "The kind of place she came from."

"We don't even know what kind of place it is," Luke said, staring down at her, wishing that she'd just stayed in Denver with her bad news and her spite.

"It's not a nice place; I know that for sure. I asked Uncle Carl about it a few days later, and he got all red in the face and had to take his glasses off and pinch his nose the way he does when he gets flustered. 'Where'd you ever hear of a place like that?' he asked, and I told him some of the kids at school were joking about it. He said that places like that were none of my business and if the mayor was half a man he'd close it down and all others like it. So it's not a good place; I know that much."

Luke said nothing, trying to pry his memory open, to find when and where he'd heard that name: Madam Floe's.

"I heard Uncle Carl and Aunt Polly talking another time—"

"Didn't you do anything else your whole time in Denver but sneak around?"

"It wasn't sneaking. I just couldn't sleep is all." She crossed her arms over her chest now, stuck out her chin. "They were talking about the strike down here and how nobody was willing to work for an honest day's wages anymore."

"They aren't honest wages," Luke said.

"That doesn't matter." Beth wagged her head at him. "But they mentioned Louis Tikas. He's from Denver. Had a coffee shop there. Did you know that?"

Ma had said as much, he remembered now, but so what? He looked at her blankly.

"Uncle Carl said the strikers should send their leaders back where they came from and return to work, and Aunt Polly laughed and said as how Tikas made a better customer at Madam Floe's than he did a strike leader. Then Uncle Carl got red in the face again and said 'Polly!' like she'd just cussed. 'You don't know that about the man.' But Aunt Polly just giggled and said, 'Well, his coffee shop *was* just next door to Floe's. What do you expect? Men like him, they can never resist temptation.'"

Beth looked at Luke with a so-there expression on her face.

It was the mention of Tikas that finally did it, that finally opened the doors to memory for Luke. It was that day at Trinidad with the gunslingers and Frankie playing the piano, and one of the miners said he hadn't heard playing like that since his last visit to Madam Floe's in

Denver. And he laughed that private laugh and his buddy joined in.

"Maybe they gamble there," Beth said. "And drink."

Luke felt his face go hot with a sudden realization. He knew what Madam Floe's was. It was the kind of place guys like Samuel Kincaid would joke about in the bathroom at recess. Samuel laughed just like those miners in Trinidad had. Luke felt the milk he was drinking go sour in his stomach. That was what the piano playing was all about: not for the movies, but for Madam Floe's. For the customers.

Easy, he told himself. Slow down. Think about it.

"So how come Aunt Polly didn't tell Ma? Answer me that one."

"Maybe she never figured it out like I did," Beth answered, still sitting there with arms crossed. "All she knows is that we got a runaway here named Francine, supposed to be from New York."

"So you're so much smarter than Aunt Polly, that it? You got it all figured out and the grown-ups are just too dumb to figure how to put their shoes on. That it?"

He began to see doubt in Beth's eyes as she looked at him sideways, not head-on.

"Maybe she does know," Beth said. "Maybe Aunt Polly told Ma. Maybe that's why they hide Frankie away here, so she doesn't go back to Denver and Madam Floe's."

Maybe, he thought. But he wasn't giving her any chances. He drove a wedge into that chink of doubt.

"You think Ma would keep anybody around here if she came from that kind of place? You've got to be crazy. You're just imagining things. So jealous that you'd figure out anything to make Frankie seem bad."

She looked downcast, but Luke himself wasn't convinced by his words. The sour taste of the milk stuck in the back of his throat. So many stories, so many turnarounds.

"You just keep your stories to yourself, Beth," he said as he was leaving. "You don't even know what you're talking about."

"I heard," she said to his back as he left the kitchen door, letting the screen door slam behind him. "I heard."

So what does it matter? he asked himself as he milked the fourth cow. The animal's steady breathing felt good as he leaned into her side. What's it matter where she played piano? She couldn't help it having to earn money. Maybe she was too embarrassed to tell him that part. And maybe Beth's story was a load of hogwash anyway.

But he knew in his bones it wasn't, knew that Frankie was connected to Madam Floe's.

So what's it matter? he asked himself again. She didn't really lie, just sort of left stuff out.

But he wasn't through with his scab yet. There was more pain to inflict by his doubts, more picking to do. So she played the piano there, but was that all? What else did she do there? How did she really get those welts on her back?

Suddenly he could hardly swallow. He felt sick and needed fresh air. Knocking over the stool, he got up and stumbled outside into the air, breathing like he'd just raced a mile.

She lied to me, he thought as he leaned against the barn door. He felt like he was on quicksand with Frankie, never knew what was true and what not. It wasn't right. Somebody should be straight with you or not at all. Like Mother Jones and her angle. Maybe that's why angles bother

Frankie so much, he thought. Because she's always play-ing one.

He took another deep breath, realizing he couldn't even ask her if it was true. What good would it do? Who could trust her? Suddenly he felt like a dummy. She'd twisted him around good. Had him believing this and that and the other. Whatever she said had to be the last bit of truth, not just another bit of lying. All was revealed. No more secrets. But there never was that last piece of truth with Frankie. Just when you thought you knew her, had her story down pat, then up popped some new piece to the puzzle.

Partners, he thought, and almost laughed out loud. That's how he'd looked at them together. But she didn't know how to make partners. The only thing Frankie knew how to make was a new story.

He wheeled around and went back into the barn, feeling lonely as a lost dog.

Luke kept it to himself, playacting now with Frankie just like she'd been doing with him. Smiling at her during dinner, letting her ride shotgun next day to school. He sat on Beth's information, trying to figure out what to do with it.

Not Beth, though. She told Janey Jones during first break, and Janey opened her big mouth and even Betty Carlson heard it by noon and started singing a stupid song as she spun around the parallel bars: "Madam Floe's is where to go, Madam Floe's is where to go."

The guys heard about it, too, and Samuel Kincaid came right up to Frankie.

"How come you don't play piano for us, Françoise?" He stretched out the final syllable of the name irritatingly.

Frankie looked from Samuel to Luke, and her eyes got

big and her lips twitched. Luke just looked at her. Miss Nielson rang the bell to end the noon break, but Billy Wilder stopped Luke as they were going back in to school.

"Is it true, Hayes? She really work at Madam Floe's? I bet you don't even know what kind of place that is, do you?"

Luke didn't bother answering. Suddenly there was not an ounce of feeling left in him, not anger at stupid Beth for opening her big mouth or even a sense of betrayal at Frankie for lying. He just felt empty and wanted life to be simple again. To do his chores and homework and not have the gnaw of doubt and of love churning his stomach in knots at night. To just be responsible for his one little patch again and not worry about what others thought of Frankie.

"It's a fancy house, Hayes," Billy Wilder went on. "Ask your pa what that means if you can't figure it out."

Luke looked at Billy and saw only a pinched-up face grinning at him, couldn't even hear his words anymore. Billy was asking for a fight, it was pretty clear, but Luke didn't swing on him, just walked slump-shouldered back into the school. He wasn't scared of Billy. It's just that there wasn't any fight left in him for Frankie.

She came to his room late that night for the last time. He didn't even roll over when he heard the door open. The floorboards creaked as she came to his bed. He could feel her standing over him.

"You believe them?" she finally said.

He kept his eyes on the wall at the side of his bed, focused on a tiny knothole in the wood that the moonlight showed him.

"So you do," she said.

He squeezed his eyes shut. He didn't want to do it

anymore, didn't want to try to figure things out all the time. He wanted to tell her that he didn't know what to believe, but by the time he finally rolled over, she was gone.

And by morning, she'd cleared out from the Hayes ranch altogether.

17

"Mighty ungrateful way to behave" was what Ma had to say of Frankie's departure. "After the way we treated her and then not even a note to say good-bye."

"We did all we could for her, Anne," Pa said after he brought back news of where Frankie was. "She'll be okay at the camp. The Thomas woman's got good character. Francine can help with her two children. Be good for her."

"Well, I suppose it'll have to be all right," Ma said. "Can't force the girl to come back. And she's got a new start now. That's the important thing. That's what we wanted for her. But it's curious she left like she did. Not a word."

Sometimes, late at night, Luke would hear the settling of the house and think it was a floorboard creaking outside his door and wait expectantly for her knock.

It never came.

March crept into April and spring was here. The last of the snow was melting off the foothills to the east, and tiny purple and gold wildflowers popped out of the arroyos and on the range out where the cattle grazed. There was such a jumble and profusion of growth brought on by the wet winter and early warm days of April that Luke felt his heart soar now when he was sent to drive the cows in for evening milking. Not a chore, but a delight.

Beth had taken to coming with him in the evening. She even managed to help out some with the animals and never once complained it was too cold or too damp or too anything. He hadn't wanted her along at first, but she'd insisted, and it turned out she hadn't been a pain in the neck. So he slowly got used to her coming along in the evening and even began to think she was okay. She kept her trap shut and did her job, which today was to stand at the edge of the big ditch and hold her arms out while Luke was driving the cows off to the left toward the barn. Cows're so dumb they'd have just tumbled down the ditch otherwise, so it was a two-man job driving them in from the east pasturage. Luke was *hee-yaw*ing the animals toward Beth and she was standing by the ditch, her little arms widespread and her hands sort of waving at them to take the turning.

The cows were making sad noises like they were being sent off to slaughter instead of to a dry stall, feed, and a good milking. They were a stubborn sort of animal and dumb as a post, but at this very minute Luke had a feeling like love for them. Nothing he wanted more than to be out here in this pasture driving the cows in with the sun sinking low in back of him over the Spanish Peaks. He guessed it'd all be his someday, this ranch. He'd be the whole show, not just doing chores, but making a living for his own family.

That thought—that someday he'd have a family of his own—opened other doors, brought the memory of Frankie back again. He'd been pretty successful keeping her out of his mind these past weeks, getting on with things. She was still at Ludlow, according to Pa, who'd caught sight of her one day, but she didn't speak to him, not even a wave of the hand.

"Something happen between you two?" Pa had asked him one night a couple weeks back. "Something maybe you want to tell me?"

"She just ran away, Pa," Luke said. "Got bored with us. It's more exciting at the camp."

Pa nodded his head like he'd heard likelier tales but didn't press him on it.

"Too bad" was all he said. "I liked Francine. Seemed like a good kid."

Sometimes Luke wondered if he shouldn't have given Frankie the chance to tell him her side, but just as quick he knew that it would have been a pack of lies. That was the problem: You never really knew Frankie's side of things. He made himself remember that now. Can't go soft on her, he told himself. She's okay at Ludlow. Maybe that's the best spot for her.

"Luke!"

Beth's yelp brought him out of his daydreaming, and he saw that he'd let the cows wander all over the place. Instead of being driven toward her, they were headed off in a dozen directions. Worst of all, a couple of them were headed for the ditch about twenty yards away from Beth.

"Get 'em!" he called to her, running toward the ditch. They go in there and they could drown with all the runoff this time of the year, he knew. Or at least break a leg tumbling down the steep bank.

Beth set off like a rabbit, shooing the cows as she ran. Luke was surprised she could move so fast. He kept running but knew he'd never get to the cows in time to head them off. The two animals were headed for the green grass at the banks of the ditch and wouldn't even see the sudden edge until it was too late.

"Go, Beth!"

She did.

"Shoo! Get out of there!" she yelled as she raced forward.

The cows had set up a pretty good clip, smelling the sweet grass now, and it would be a close thing, Luke could see. Just as he thought she wouldn't make it, Beth put on a burst of speed that would've impressed every guy at school. The cows veered off track just as they reached the edge of the bank, but Beth kept going, tumbling out of sight.

"Beth!"

Luke got to the edge in time to see one of her arms waving frantically out of the water, but her head was underneath. He didn't stop to think but dove right in. When he hit the water, he remembered he couldn't swim a lick. He didn't panic, though, and his feet hit slimy bottom and held, his head just above the water line. Beth exploded out of the water in front of him, her eyes big and scared, and then she went under again just as quick. Luke managed to jab a hand out and catch her wrist. The water was flowing through the ditch pretty fast. Rivers were high with the early melt from the mountains. But he managed to hold on, to move back to the bank without slipping and going under himself. Soon he'd moved far enough toward the lower bank that the footing was steady and he could drag her up and out. She was spitting water and coughing like crazy as he laid her on her back on the muddy ledge.

"You almost drowned, Beth." He was panting pretty good himself.

"Yeah," she said, catching her breath and propping herself up on her elbows. "I sort of figured that out."

They both laughed.

"You're crazy," he said.

"Well, you told me to catch them."

He rubbed her wet hair. "I didn't tell you to kill yourself doing it."

"It's a good thing you can swim," she said, still breathing hard.

"Yeah," he said, not bothering to inform her otherwise. "I guess it is."

"Besides," Beth said. "I don't know what Pa would've done if anything happened to the cows. He told us three times to be careful with the ditch."

"It was my fault," Luke said. "Sorry. I wasn't thinking."

"Probably thinking too much." She smiled at him. "Thanks for pulling me out. We won't tell Pa, okay? Just say we slipped getting the gate open or something."

"You're a good kid sister, Beth." He helped her to her feet, and hand in hand they crawled back up the steep slope to the pasturage. The two cows were munching grass happily and looked up startled as Luke and Beth elbowed their way onto the top of the ditch.

They got along better after that. No more of the little bratty sister. Luke didn't even mind walking up to the school with her. And it pleased Ma, Luke knew, to see them so friendly with one another. The weather held clear, too, and the cows were milking good. The world should have been an all-right place to be.

But for Luke, after that day in the pasture and the way Frankie had come back into his mind, the spring suddenly stopped. He didn't see the wildflowers anymore, didn't enjoy dinner, couldn't even take heart from the prospect of summer vacation coming up.

Time had played tricks on Luke. He had forgotten the slippery feeling of quicksand Frankie engulfed him in. The bite of doubt had softened into the sepia of nostalgia. He started to think he'd made a big mistake about

141

Frankie. He really *should* have given her the chance to at least hear Beth's story. But he hadn't, and that ate at him. He hadn't been fair with her, and he knew it. They'd had good times together, and he just cut and ran. Leastwise, that's the way he began to look at it now. He couldn't sleep at night, couldn't concentrate in school, couldn't even be tempted by Ma's apple crumble.

"You sick, Luke?" Beth asked one day after dinner while they were doing the washing up.

"Nope." He was washing; she was drying.

"You don't look good, and you never even finish your meals."

"Not hungry."

"Come on, Luke. You can tell me. It's her, isn't it? Frankie."

He could never get the tea stain out of the teapot, had given up even trying, but he made sure that the outside was clean. Ma checked.

The water in the sink sloshed as he washed. Silverware clinked as Beth dried it directly into the drawer.

"I'm sorry I was so awful about her," she finally said. "But I missed you. I felt like I was cut off from everybody. Maybe I just did the cutting off myself."

He looked at her and smiled. "Where'd you start getting so smart? Can't be Aunt Polly's doing."

"Maybe you ought to go see Frankie."

"I thought you hated her."

Beth dried the big bowl with extra care. Ma had brought it all the way from Rapid City with her.

"It's better now," she said. "I mean she's your friend. What do I care?"

"Sure. Besides, I don't know if she ever really was my friend." He almost stopped himself. He had never talked this way with Beth before, like with a best friend. But he

142

needed somebody to talk to, somebody to hear. "I mean," he said, finishing with the washing and letting the water out of the sink with a gurgle and whoosh, "I never knew, did I? She had so many stories."

"Luke?"

"Yeah."

"You promise you won't get mad?"

He dried his hands on a dishrag. "What?"

"Promise?"

"Okay."

"Well, I sort of lied."

"What do you mean?"

"You promised."

He reined in his anger. "Okay. Lied about what? Madam Floe's?"

She shook her head fiercely. "I really did hear all that." She looked up at him with determined eyes. "It was something else. Before I left for Denver. Remember on the platform at Ludlow?"

He nodded, trying to figure out where this was going.

"And I told you Frankie was trying to buy my friendship with all those gifts, the candy and all? Well . . ."

"Come on."

"Remember your promise."

He knew. "They really were for me, weren't they?" he said.

"Yup." She looked at her feet. "I saw her put them at your door. I would've stolen them, but I was afraid you'd catch me at it." She looked up and there were tears in her eyes. "I'm sorry, Luke. Sorry I did it. But I just felt so bad. Felt like nobody liked me anymore."

He pulled her to his side, putting an arm over her shoulder and patting her. It was as affectionate as he'd ever got with her.

She sobbed, then looked up at him.

"You aren't mad?"

"I'm glad you told me."

"You going to go see her?"

"Maybe."

18

It was the Saturday before Easter by the time he could get to Ludlow, and then he had to sneak there, jumping a train at the water tower like Frankie had taught him to. But he didn't bother getting inside, just dropped off the back car as soon as it began to slow down to pull into the Ludlow station. Good thing he got off early because the platform was packed with soldiers in full gear, and they began crowding on the train the minute it stopped.

He saw Captain van Cise on the platform with a couple duffel bags at his feet, and he was checking off men as they got onto the train. Luke walked right up to him.

"Hi, Captain," he said. "What's going on?"

Van Cise smiled when he looked up from the list and saw Luke.

"Well, hello. You hopping trains again?"

"No. Pa dropped me off on the way to deliver milk."

Van Cise nodded and grinned more broadly. "Guess that's why your hair's blown all over the place. Truck's a windy means of transport."

Luke automatically smoothed down his mat of hair, feeling his face redden at being caught out in a lie.

"You leaving?" he said.

"That's about the size of it. Troop strength is being reduced here. Strike seems about finished, so what's the use?"

"But they're still in the camp, aren't they?" Luke cast a glance and saw the tent city.

"Oh, yes. Still there. And the mines are still operating at full production. The strikers lost, son. Just nobody told them so yet. We got wives and children waiting for us back home. Can't play soldier forever."

"But what's going to happen to them?" Luke realized he'd all but forgotten the strikers, so caught up had he been with his own problems.

Van Cise shook his head. "Who knows? Tikas has got his hands full, though. Lots of angry men in that camp, in all the camps around Trinidad and Walsenburg. That Luigi, his second-in-command, he and lots of others think Tikas has been too soft. That it's his fault the strike isn't working. Wouldn't take much to set those men off."

"Then you ought to be staying."

Van Cise had gone back to checking his list but looked up at this comment.

"Orders," he said, and a muscle twitched in his jaw. "You going to the camp?"

Luke nodded. "Got some business."

"Well, you say good-bye to Mr. Tikas for me. He's a good man. But tell him to watch his back. They aren't all good men. Not on either side of this."

Luke stood for a moment longer on the platform, feeling a sort of sinking in his stomach as he watched Captain van Cise's men board the train. They were good guys, friends, sort of. They'd worked together digging the camp out, had played baseball with the strikers. Didn't take sides. Now they were going, and Frankie's words came back to Luke: Once van Cise leaves, then you've got Linderfelt and the gun-happy Greeks staring at each other, just itching for a fight. And for what?

Finally the men had all boarded, van Cise the last to get

146

on, tossing his duffel bags up first and then mounting the steps lightly.

"You remember what I said," he called to Luke as the train began pulling out. "And say good-bye to Mrs. Thomas for me, too."

Luke nodded his head at him and waved. The train gave a long, sad hoot as it clacked over the steel bridge north of town and then was gone out of sight around a bend.

He jumped down off the platform and was heading for the camp when he spotted her, dressed in dungarees and the old mackinaw and a cap, and looking like a boy if you didn't watch real close the sort of loose-limbed way she moved from the hips. Frankie didn't see him, and he followed her, not wanting to call out, wanting to surprise her. He smiled, feeling good just to see her again.

She went into the post office next to the depot, but that wasn't her destination. She was out the back door even as he entered the front, and from a window of the post office he watched as she scampered through sagebrush and cut to her right, going south. He went out the back and was going to call out to her, but there was something strange about the way she was sneaking off, lighting out the back of the post office like she didn't want anybody tailing her. So Luke didn't say anything. Just followed.

She moved fast through the sagebrush and up a little hill that overlooked the station. Luke stayed well in back and kept quiet. Luckily, there was some taller brush here to give him cover, because Frankie looked back a couple of times just to make sure nobody was following, making him even more curious. His mouth went dry with a thought: Maybe she was meeting some guy, like at Madam Floe's. *If* that was really her from Madam Floe's. Beth had been lying about the candy. Why not figure she was laying it on thick with all that Denver stuff, too?

But he had no time to think further, for at that moment a figure appeared out of the brush near the top of the hill, and Frankie went right up to him.

Linderfelt.

Luke tried to make himself invisible in the brush, watching from his cover all that went on. Frankie didn't look scared of him, and Linderfelt didn't look as mean as usual, either. He nodded at her like he was expecting her and they talked for a while. Frankie waved a hand back down toward the camp a couple of times, like she was explaining something. Linderfelt looked at her pretty close, as much as Luke could make out. Nodded his head a couple more times. Frankie kept looking around her like she wanted to get out of there pronto. Linderfelt said something more and then she talked. Finally he pulled a wallet out of his pants pockets and slipped a couple bills out of it and handed them to her. She stuffed them in the right front pocket of her dungarees and then headed off back down the hill toward Luke. He hugged the ground as she passed, not breathing, not making a move.

She passed by him, making no sign that she saw him. No hesitation to her step, and her booted feet were all Elmo could see from the underbrush.

He let out a silent sigh.

"Meet me at the station in five minutes," she whispered at him over her shoulder. "And don't let Linderfelt see you."

She was waiting on the front steps of the station, just by the refuse can where he'd thrown away the badge several months earlier. Her hands were dug into the pockets of the mackinaw, and her cap was pulled down low over her eyes. He came and sat down beside her, not saying a word. They sat like that for a couple of minutes, like playing a game of stare-down, until he finally gave in.

"Okay," he said. "Just what's going on?"

She looked straight ahead of her feet, where a parade of ants was crossing the dusty floorboards of the bottom step, carrying home little chunks of something white as bounty. She leaned over and blew into the column, knocking a few of the ants out of line, sending them tumbling down off the step. But others behind quickly filled in the missing places, and it was like those other ants never even existed.

"I said what the heck's going on?"

She squinted up at him, tipping the cap back on her forehead.

"You taken to snooping just like your kid sister?"

"I wasn't snooping. I came . . ." But he couldn't say it now, couldn't wrangle up the apology with her squinting anger at him.

"You came for what?"

"Nothing."

He watched the ant column, wishing he'd never left the ranch, never let himself in for such confusion again.

She broke the silence this time. "So you want to know about Linderfelt and me?"

He nodded, not looking at her.

"Why should I tell you? What're you to me?"

He didn't have an answer to that one. Suddenly, for no good reason, he stomped at the line of ants, squashing a good dozen of them. A few of the ants were crawling up his dusty boot as he lifted it. Others were stumbling and limping away, still others scurrying around like messengers of doom. But again the line closed on itself.

He felt mean and stupid all at once, but Frankie only sighed and stood up.

"Ask Tikas if you want to know. He's the one set it up."

She jumped down over the ant step and didn't bother waving good-bye as she strode back to the camp.

*　　*　　*

149

He wasn't sure how long he sat on those depot steps, maybe half an hour, maybe an hour. It was like he was dreaming. Finally he determined to get to the bottom of things, to find out once and for all about Frankie.

Ask Tikas, she'd said. Well, Luke thought, no time like the present.

The camp population had thinned out some since his last visit. Lots of the families were gone now, and there were more single men than before. No longer were bunches of little kids running around the compound playing tag. Luke headed straight for Tikas's tent.

"Hey, Luke."

He didn't slow down as Frank Snyder ran to catch up with him.

"What're you up to?"

Luke half nodded at him. He wasn't in any mood to joke around.

"Got to see Tikas," he said as he kept on moving.

"What about?"

"Got some business to talk about."

"Gonna be sort of hard to do that," Frank said, stretching his shorter legs to keep up with Luke.

"How's that?"

"He's gone to Trinidad for a couple days."

Luke stopped dead in his tracks. Sudden anger swept over him. It was always like this when he was trying to find out the truth about Frankie.

He suddenly spun around on the smaller kid.

"Can't you ever be serious? Why not just tell me the man isn't here?"

Frank looked up at him with surprise. Red splotches formed in the hollows of his cheeks.

"Hey, I was just playing around."

"That's what I mean. It's not always a game."

And he pushed past Frank and headed out of the camp for the long walk home.

The next Friday Pa took sick with a pain in his side that laid him low and brought Doc Marlow out to the ranch again. The doc said it was a gall bladder attack, but giving it a name didn't do anything to relieve Pa's pain.

"Must have been those chocolates we got in for Easter last Sunday," Ma said. "Somebody ate more than their fair share of them."

They were all gathered in the sickroom, and Ma cut her eyes at Pa in bed, looking pretty green in the face. Just the mention of chocolates made him groan some more.

"Could be chocolates," Doc Marlow said, "could be too much bacon. Who knows. But the important thing is we get him some relief."

He left a bottle of morphine, and Pa slept pretty good after that. Saturday was a rough day, and Sunday Pa was a little better but in no condition to go to the camp. Luke and Beth took care of the outdoor chores on their own. They'd had to skip the milk run the last couple days; looked like they'd have to get Mr. Green from the neighboring farm to deliver their milk along with his own tomorrow. Pa had tried to teach Ma how to drive once, but she didn't take to it and quit after a few attempts at the intricacies of gear-shifting. She always said she could drive in an emergency, but milk deliveries didn't fit her idea of emergency. Luke wasn't allowed to drive yet—even though he swore to Ma he could handle it.

All in all, it was a quiet sort of day and early to bed. Luke and Beth needed to get up extra early so they'd have time to walk out to the main road and catch the school bus. No ride from Pa in the morning.

It must've been two or three when he awoke from a

151

dreamless sleep, not knowing why at first. Then there was another clatter of dirt clods at his window. He got up and went to it, looking down into the yard. Not much to see without the moon. Then another bunch of tiny clods hit the window, making him jump back for a moment. He opened the window, stuck his head out.

"Luke." A loud whisper in the night.

He looked down just below him and saw her. It took him about half a minute to slip on his dungarees and shirt and shoes without socks because he couldn't find them in the darkness and then get downstairs without sounding the big creak on step twelve and out the front door, making sure the door didn't slam in back of him.

She was there on the front porch, her hands struck into the mackinaw, the cap on her head stuck down low over her ears so that she looked more like a boy than a girl.

"Come on." She moved to the steps. "They might hear."

He followed her toward the barn, a million questions going through his mind.

"What you doing back here?" was all he could say, and this stopped her just in front of the barn.

She whirled around on him suddenly. "Tell your pa not to make his delivery tomorrow."

"Why not? Is that why you came?"

"Never mind why not; just stay away."

It was like she was a different person now, older. Smarter. Playing by different rules.

"What's going on, Frankie?"

His eyes were adjusting to the darkness now, and he could see her face more clearly. It looked like there was a bruise on her cheek, but she was just grinning at him like she always did when he was being dumb.

"Where'd you get that?" he said, pointing at her cheek.

"Boy, you're full of questions, Luke. Why don't you just listen for once? Have your pa stay away tomorrow. That's all I'm telling you. Those people at Ludlow, if they were smart they'd get out of there like I told them."

"It's Linderfelt, isn't it? He's got something planned. Did he do that to you?"

"Always want to find out everything, don't you, Luke? Every last little detail. Someday I guess you'll figure out you can't. That some things just don't come down to yes–no. I'm headed out of here. Saved up my money." She gave a little laugh. "Amazing how much both sides pay you to tell them what they already know. But if they want to give me money for it, that's okay by me."

She brought out a wad of bills from her jacket pocket.

"How you figure it, Luke? That's what they pay me for *not* making it yes–no, for being in the middle of it, on both sides."

"But whose side are you really on?" Luke asked. "Who are you for?"

"Me, of course. If you were smart, that's where you'd be, too."

She stuck the money back in her jacket pocket. "Remember what I told you; keep him away from the camp tomorrow."

She turned to go. He didn't bother to tell her his pa was so laid up he couldn't go on his milk run anyway.

"Frankie. Where you headed?"

She looked back over her shoulder.

"Places," she said. "Just places."

He let her go. There was no stopping her anyway.

19

It was almost first light by the time he reached the camp. A pearly gray line edged in pink showed over the eastern horizon. Early-morning breeze was up, carrying the scent of sage and coal dust.

Suddenly, in this morning light, his mission seemed pretty silly. A few of the strikers were up already, throwing water in their faces from galvanized washbasins. One man was shaving by the side of his tent. Somebody even had wash on the line, swaying easy in the morning breeze. The Stars and Stripes was ruffling in the same breeze from the pole at the entrance, and there was a whistling coming from the main tent: somebody getting breakfast ready, bacon scent in the air.

Maybe this was a stupid errand after all, Luke thought as he came through the entrance. Maybe Frankie was just exaggerating so she'd feel better about hopping it out of here.

"Why, Luke. You're early. Where's your pa?"

It was Mary Thomas, just coming out of the communal tent and headed back to her own.

"He couldn't come," Luke said, suddenly feeling awfully dumb.

She looked at him with a puzzled expression.

"He's sick," Luke added.

"I'm sorry to hear that." The questioning gaze grew

154

more pronounced on her face as she looked around for their delivery truck.

Luke remembered another errand, and he came out with it now to cover his confusion: "I saw Captain van Cise last week," he said, "Told me to tell you good-bye."

"Well, that was nice of him. But you didn't come all the way here just to tell me that, did you?"

"No, ma'am."

But before he could tell her why he did come, three militiamen rode up to the camp, reined in their horses just by the entrance, and then one of them rode in alone, scowling at the tents.

"Tikas around?" he said gruffly to Mary Thomas.

"Yes. What do you men want?"

"Just get me Tikas, lady."

She looked at Luke. "He's in the headquarters tent over there. Get him, will you?"

She stayed with the soldier as Luke raced to the tent.

"Mr. Tikas," he called from outside. "Somebody wants you."

Tikas popped his bare head out of the tent. "Luke. What are you doing here?" Luke could see that Tikas wasn't dressed yet, was still in his nightwear.

Luke pointed over to the militiaman. "He asked for you."

Tikas looked at the soldier. "Just a moment."

When he came out of the tent a little bit later, Tikas had on his jacket and black-and-white checked cap. He strode over to the horseman and gestured Mary Thomas away politely.

They talked for a while, the soldier waving around the camp like he was in charge and Tikas replying softly but firmly. Finally the militiaman wheeled his horse and headed away from the camp, followed by the other two soldiers.

Tikas walked back to Mary Thomas. By this time the other strikers had been alerted that something was going on. Luigi was out, a revolver stuck into the waist of his pants.

"What is it?" Luigi said.

Tikas shook his head in disgust. "They say we are holding a miner against his will. An Italian named Pardone." He looked at Luigi. "Do we have such a man here?"

Luigi shook his head. "They're just looking for a reason to fight."

Tikas held a hand up for silence. "We should make sure, all the same."

Luke watched the men gathering in the middle of the camp. He still wondered if Frankie had told Tikas whatever it was that had scared her off. But his thoughts were halted now, as he realized that these men weren't the pleasant-faced miners he'd known from before. Now there was a bitter cast on their faces. Many carried guns. Not just revolvers, either, but rifles and shotguns. Supposedly all weapons had been collected by the National Guard troops, but there obviously were secret caches. The tents were emptying of men.

"I tell you, Tikas," Luigi said, "we have no person of that name. But if they want a fight over it, we'll give them one."

Suddenly Luke knew Frankie's warning was not an exaggeration. She'd known exactly what was going to happen today.

"You better get on home, Luke," Mary Thomas said. He'd forgotten she was still at his side, so involved was he in watching the men.

He looked at her. She was so tiny, shorter than him. And with her two kids, what was she going to do?

"You staying?" he said.

156

"I live here."

"Then so am I."

A man yelled out from the command tent: "Call for Tikas. It's the soldier boys."

Tikas went to the tent, his face drawn and lips puckered. After a few minutes, he came out again.

"They want me to meet with them," he announced to the gathered men.

"Linderfelt?" Luigi asked.

"No," Tikas shook his head. "Major Hamrock. At the depot. Neutral ground."

"Hell with them," one of the men said.

Tikas looked at Luigi. "What do you say?"

Luigi scratched his cheek. "Maybe it's worth a try."

Luke wanted to shout out to Tikas not to go, wanted to voice Captain van Cise's warning to him about Luigi. But it was too late.

"That's what I thought," Tikas said. "You men remain calm. I'll be back shortly."

They watched him walk toward the depot alone and unarmed, looking very small in the flat bowl of Ludlow. He wasn't more than fifty yards from camp when Luigi ordered the men to split into two companies and fan out into the arroyos to the east and west of the camp, to encircle the troops stationed in both areas.

"They are only a handful of men. We are many. We strike now before they bring more troops in."

"Tikas said to stay calm," Mary Thomas protested.

Luigi grinned, holding out a steady hand. "You see. I remain calm."

The men laughed nervously.

"He doesn't want you to fight," Luke said. "He's trying to make a deal."

But the men ignored him. They did as Luigi ordered and

157

spread out of the camp in both directions, hunkered down low and using the tents to cover their movement.

"You got to get your kids out of here, Mrs. Thomas," Luke said. "There's going to be trouble for sure."

No sooner had he said it than shooting began. The militia had obviously noticed the encircling movement of the strikers and opened fire on them. There were only a few shots at first, sharp and echoing in the early morning. The shots turned into a volley, then a roar as men shot nonstop from both sides.

Those in the camp—mostly women and children—stood immobile for a moment, staring at one another, at the depot where Tikas had disappeared. The battle was elsewhere, but the noise was deafening. Suddenly Tikas came bolting out of the depot, waving his hands wildly toward those in the camp to stop shooting, but the fighters were outside now and could not see him. Tikas drew militia fire, bullets kicking dirt at his heels as he ran. And suddenly the bullets were tearing through the canvas tents in the camp, breaking crockery, pinging off the washing tubs. Luke heard a fly buzz by his ear and realized it was a bullet. He grabbed Mary Thomas and pulled her to the ground with him.

"We got to get out of here," he yelled.

"My children!"

"Where are they?"

Tikas stumbled into the camp, screaming at the women and children to find cover, to get into their earthen holes under the floorboards or run to the safety of the pump station.

Luke and Mary Thomas crawled on hands and knees to her tent, where her children were crying and huddled by the bed. A bullet ripped through the tent, tearing canvas but hitting nothing. They gathered the children in their

158

arms, and Mary Thomas was about to take along a picture of her family in Wales.

"Leave it," Luke said. "You need to move fast."

She looked around the tent for a moment and then they went out again, the children wiggling in their arms in terror. Other people in the camp were crawling into their hidey-holes or gathering up their belongings and scampering for the pump station.

"I should try to help them," Mary Thomas said. "Some of the women have young children."

Outside, Tikas was running from tent to tent to check on the people and literally bumped into Luke.

"How did this start?" Tikas was frantic. "I told them to stay calm."

"Luigi," Luke said.

Tikas shook his head. "I should have known. I should have listened to Frankie."

The child Luke was carrying was sobbing in his ear, but he felt a sudden expansion in his lungs, a lightness in his head. So Frankie did warn them, he thought. She didn't just run away from her friends at the first sign of danger. But Tikas hadn't believed her, hadn't taken her seriously.

No time for regrets now, though. Another round of fire tore into the camp, but this time it was different—regular, continuous. Not the pop and crack of rifle and small-arms fire. It made Tikas's eyes go wide. A man running across the compound took two rounds in his leg and tumbled head over heels, to lie moaning near the communal tent.

"The gun," Tikas said as he ran to help the wounded man. "They have the gun. Get underground or out of the camp!"

Luke knew what he meant. It was the Gatling gun he and Frankie had seen on the train that day. Linderfelt.

Suddenly from directly behind them came a wailing and

crying. Mr. Snyder stumbled out of his tent, his wife behind him, holding her head in her hands and screaming. In one arm Snyder carried his young daughter; over his shoulder was slung a body.

No, Luke thought. Don't let it be so.

"They killed my boy. Killed my boy" was all Snyder could get out.

Snyder plowed on blindly through the camp, in the direction of the station. Blood coated the back of his shirt. Luke made himself look at the body: Frank Snyder's head had been blown apart by a bullet. Luke felt a sudden sickness catch at his throat.

Mary Thomas was the first to react. "I have to help," she said. "You take the children. Go to the pump house."

Luke was already carrying one child, and now she put the second in his arms. He was numb from seeing Frank dead like that. All he could think of was the last time he'd seen Frank, the hard words he'd used. He didn't know what to do for a moment, just stood there holding both the crying children.

"Please," she said. "Save my children." She half pushed him in the direction of the pump house, only a hundred yards or so from the tent colony. Her urging made him come alive. He could do nothing for Frank, but he could at least make sure that Mary's kids were safe.

They were heavy in his arms, and finally he had to set them down and hold on firmly to their hands as he ran. They kept looking around at their mother, who was kneeling by a wounded man now, and yelling for her. Finally Luke dragged them, screaming, the last twenty yards to the small wooden shack.

The militia had not homed in on this position yet, and it was full of families and screaming babies, jam-packed so that Luke could hardly open the door to get in.

160

"You'll have to go elsewhere," a man was telling the people. By the look of his blue cap, he worked for the railway, probably operated the pump station, Luke figured.

"These walls won't keep bullets out," he said.

"And where can we go?" one woman bawled at him. "It's a battleground out there."

The man looked at all the huddled people, thought for a moment, then snapped his fingers.

"The deep well," he said. "You went by it coming from the camp. It's cold and damp, but she's made of concrete, and there are platforms inside where you can stand. It'll be safe there. Safer than here."

The women looked doubtful, but Luke could see it was a good idea.

"Come on," Luke said. "Concrete's better than wood."

He led them, probably fifty women and children, to the well, and they looked over the edge. A foul stench came up at them from the bottom.

"I'm not going down there," a woman with a baby in her arms said.

Just then the spray of bullets from the Gatling gun reached the pump station, splintering its wooden walls.

"Well, you're not going back there either," Luke said and hefted the Thomas girls over the side to the first platform. He went over himself then. There were metal ladders leading to the other platforms, and they seemed to be steady enough.

"Come on," he urged the others, and finally they all crawled over the lip of the well and spread out onto the platforms. It was cramped and cold, but at least bullets couldn't get to them down here.

Most of the day they listened to the battle as it raged to the east and then the west and back to the east. Children cried, then slept, then woke to cry again. Luke crouched down to hold Mary Thomas's little girls close to him, to warm them and comfort them.

"It'll be okay," he kept saying. "Your ma will be here soon."

"Is your ma out there, too?" one of the girls finally asked him.

"No. My ma's at home," he told her.

"She's lucky, huh?"

"Sure," he said.

Bullets sometimes hit the concrete lip of the well, sending dust and fragments below, but nobody got injured. Just scared out of their wits.

"Maybe we ought to sing," one of the women finally said. And she started a hymn that the English-speaking ones knew, but not the Italian women. They'd just hum along. Then the Italian women sang together and the others hummed. Luke whistled along with all of the songs, happy for anything to take his mind off what was going on outside and to make him blot out the vision of Frank Snyder's body dangling over his father's shoulder. . . .

It was late afternoon when new arrivals came. Luke looked up as the two scampered down the ladder toward his platform. He right away saw the shock of red hair, and his heart took off.

"Mrs. Thomas!"

She looked down. "God bless you, Luke. You've kept them safe."

He looked at the second figure coming down the ladder above Mrs. Thomas and recognized the old mackinaw before he could see her face. He didn't say anything as she descended. Mary Thomas embraced her two children, smothering them with kisses.

Frankie took the last rung slowly, looking Luke square in the eye.

162

"Don't say 'You've come back.' Okay?"

He shook his head, a smile on his face. "I promise I won't."

He kept looking at her until she stuck her hands in her pockets in frustration.

"Okay," she said. "I came back. So quit staring."

"Must've missed your train, that it?" he said.

"Yeah." She shrugged, looking around the dank walls of the well. "Heard there was a great party at the camp I shouldn't ought to miss."

It was growing dark outside now, and still the shooting continued. Frankie and Luke huddled close together in the press of bodies on the platform. He could feel the warmth of her next to him.

Finally a man's voice sounded from above.

"You all right down there?"

It was Tikas and another man, the camp paymaster, looking down the well.

"Fair to middling," Mary Thomas called back. "Can we come out of here?"

"Not yet. When it gets dark enough, we'll take you out. For now, you are safest where you are."

Suddenly the black opening of the well was illuminated in orange light.

"Louis!" the other man with Tikas said. "They're torching the camp."

Another voice called out from nearby: "Tikas! Louis Tikas. You hear?"

The voice had an echo sound, like it was being funneled through a megaphone. But even with that, Luke could recognize it. Linderfelt.

"I hear," Tikas called back. "You must stop the fire. There are women and children in the camp still."

"You want to stop it, you come talk."

Tikas looked down the well.

163

"Don't do it, Louis," Mary Thomas shouted.

"You talk, we put the fire out," Linderfelt shouted.

Tikas looked down at all of the women and children crowded on the platforms and smiled at them. Then, looking off to his left, where Linderfelt's voice was coming from, he cupped his hands to his mouth and called out: "I'm coming to talk."

"No!" Frankie grabbed Luke's wrist. "They'll kill him for sure." She began scrambling up the ladder, but Luke took hold of her leg.

"Let go," she said. "I got to stop him. Tell him that's what Linderfelt wants. That's his plan."

"I'll come with you then," Luke said.

But she shook her head. "No. You got to stay here. Understand?"

"I'm going with you."

She gave him that look of hers again, that glance that said wise up.

"Don't you get it? You can't go. Your job is to stay here, to help the women get out later tonight when it's dark. You know the country. There are more strikers to the north in the big arroyo. I passed them coming here. You'll be safe there. You got to do it, Luke. Besides, you want your ma to lose two sons to the mines? Do you? It'd kill her."

He looked at her for a long moment, felt the tough sinew at her ankle where he held her.

"Hey," she said, smiling. "It'll be okay. I'll be right back. You'll see."

"Linderfelt will kill you if he sees you."

"His bark's worse than his bite," she said. "Now let go."

Luke's hand trailed away, and she scampered up the ladder and over the lip of the well and was gone.

"She'll be back," Mary Thomas said to him. "She's a survivor."

But she didn't come back, and the fire finally burned itself out at the camp. When it was pitch-black outside, Luke led the Thomas family and the other women and children out of the well, just as Frankie had told him he must do. Led them north, toward the wide arroyo, past the fighting, past the killing. In back of them, the Ludlow camp smoldered like embers in an untended fireplace.

Other strikers were gathering in the arroyo, reinforcements from Walsenburg and Hastings. And wives looking for husbands, even some of the local people come to give help and food. Amid them all was Ma, her hair pulled every which way out of her usual neatly braided bun and grabbing every new arrival to look at them up close. She hugged Luke for a long moment when she finally found him. He could hear her sobs, feel them as she pressed him to her.

"We got to get Frankie," he said finally, pushing himself at arm's length from her. "She went with Tikas. We got to find her."

But Ma just shook her head, her eyes flooded with tears.

"We're going home, Luke. Nothing more we can do here. Nothing more we can do for Francine."

"She's out there, Ma," Luke pleaded. "She needs us."

Ma continued to shake her head, and finally her words sank in.

"But Frankie's a survivor," he said through sudden tears. "Everybody says so. She'll be out there hiding somewhere, waiting for help."

"In the morning, son," Ma said. "Nothing to be done when it's dark. We're going home now. Going home."

He looked back helplessly toward the camp. All he could see was a faint orange glow. The occasional pop of rifle fire sounded in the hollow hills. Here in the arroyo people were sharing food and news, the women finding out from other strikers where their men were, getting the word on casualties and small victories.

"She came back," Luke finally said.

"I know." Ma put out a soft hand to his face, cupping his cheek for a moment, then sniffed once and stood ramrod straight. "Like you say, she's a survivor. And she came back in the end. That's the important part. All the rest, well, that just doesn't count."

Luke looked at her for a moment, wondering how much Ma knew about all the stories, wondering if any of them would ever know the truth about Frankie. Then he suddenly realized Ma was right. It didn't matter. The lies, the unanswered questions. Where Frankie came from and why. What side she was on. None of it mattered. In the end, she came back. That's what counted.

She came back.

Epilogue

In the morning a telephone linesman was going through the charred remains of the Ludlow camp and found the bodies: eleven children and four women, who had been caught underground when the fire was started by the militia. The smoke had asphyxiated them.

This event became known as the Ludlow Massacre. It not only rallied national opinion against the mine operators and the Rockefeller interests but also brought armed supporters out in the hills of southern Colorado. Real warfare broke out thereafter and continued until President Woodrow Wilson called in the federal troops. When the dust and smoke cleared, sixty-six men, women, and children on both sides had died. The strike was broken. However, not one mine guard or militiaman was indicted for a crime.

While the story of Ludlow is a true one and most of the incidents and main characters in this book are historical, Luke and Frankie, along with the Hayes family, are inventions.

Louis Tikas and James Fyler, paymaster for the strikers, were found dead the same day the fifteen women and children were uncovered. The militia claimed both men had been shot while trying to escape custody.

A third body was said to have been found near theirs, that of a young boy, sprawled along the Ludlow tracks. The militia buried the body in an unmarked grave. It was never identified.

About the Author

J. SYDNEY JONES, a freelance writer, is the author of seven adult books of both fiction and nonfiction, among them *The Hero Game* and *Time of the Wolf*, published by New American Library. He enjoys listening to Celtic and baroque music, hiking, and playing tennis. Mr. Jones lives in Aptos, California, with his daughter, Tess.